CHAPTER ONE
TROUBLE

The vein in Principal Purvis's head looked as though it was about to explode. It ran from the top of his hairless head to the beginning of his nose and was growing larger as his face grew redder. It was incredible. I had seen it before—but never this big. And he didn't even know about the broken glass and smashed goldfish yet.

"Pappenfuss! What in the world are you looking at?"

"Uh . . . just the time, sir."

Mr. Purvis pointed above my head. "The clock, Mr. Pappenfuss, is on the wall behind you!"

I laughed nervously and thanked him. We shared an awkward moment before he continued. "Peter Paul Pappenfuss, this is the second time in two weeks you have been sent to my office. And school has been in session for only two weeks!"

Unfortunately, he was right on all three accounts. He was right that this was my second time to the principal's office; he was right that school had started only two weeks ago; and he was right that my name is Peter Paul Pappenfuss. The reason for my ridiculous nomenclature has to do with my parents (my dad, specifically) being the pastors of First Church in Davenport, Iowa—home of the Figge Art Museum as well as Happy Joe's Jungle Bungle.

My parents wanted me to have a Bible name, but they couldn't agree what that name should be. So because they were both stubborn, I was blessed with two biblical names.

"Peter Paul, are you listening to me?" demanded Principal Purvis.

"Absolutely, sir."

"Are you? Then what did I just say?"

"Uh . . . why? Did you forget?"

Mr. Purvis ran his fingers over his sweaty bald head and exhaled loudly. "Peter Paul, you are one of the most exasperating students in this school! As a matter of fact, I think that whole fifth-grade class of yours is out to kill me this year. They've all been inspired by your antics at the camporee a few weeks ago. It's a wonder you didn't kill anybody."

"But that wasn't my fault!" I protested.

"SILENCE!" roared Mr. Purvis. "I suppose that plane drove itself?" He took a deep breath and leaned forward across his oak desk, licked his lips, and looked me dead in the eye—speaking very deliberately. "But you won't succeed, young man. None of you will."

Principal Purvis turned to the watercooler in the corner of his little office for a drink. After three cupfuls of water, he calmed down. He has the shortest fuse of anybody I have ever met. Almost anything sends him over the edge, and it doesn't help that he's our music teacher.

Our school's musical talent is the equivalent of a group of monkeys banging toasters together. Everyone hates it—including Principal Purvis. It drives him up the wall, and class usually ends with him telling us all to *"BE QUIET!"*—something the other teachers scold him for.

Principal Purvis sat back down in his chair and looked at me coolly. "I hope I'm not coming off too harsh, Peter Paul, but this is turning out to be a stressful day." It was *always* a stressful day for Principal Purvis. "Now, let's start from the beginning," he continued. "Tell me what happened."

"I . . . um . . ."

"Just tell me, Son. I promise I'll try not to get too upset." I knew he would get upset, but I also knew I wouldn't be able to leave his office until I told. I had no choice but to talk.

"Well, Sam Feltzer was leaning back on his chair, and Harley O'Brien suggested that I kick one of the legs that wasn't resting on the floor. So I did, and—"

"And he fell over?" prompted Principal Purvis, thinking that was all.

THE MISADVENTURES OF PETER PAUL PAPPENFUSS

THE DAY THE SCHOOL BLEW UP

SETH J. PIERCE

Pacific Press® Publishing Association
Nampa, Idaho
Oshawa, Ontario, Canada
www.pacificpress.com

Cover design by Gerald Lee Monks
Cover illustration by Marcus Mashburn
Interior design by Aaron Troia

Additional copies of this book are available by calling toll-free 1-800-765-6955 or
by visiting www.adventistbookcenter.com

Unless otherwise noted, Scripture quotations are from The New King James
Version, copyright © 1979, 1980, 1982, Thomas Nelson, Inc., Publishers.

Scripture quotations marked NIV are from the HOLY BIBLE, NEW
INTERNATIONAL VERSION®. Copyright © 1973, 1978, 1984 by International
Bible Society. Used by permission of Zondervan Publishing House. All rights
reserved.

Library of Congress Cataloging-in-Publication Data

Pierce, Seth J.
  The day the school blew up / Seth J. Pierce.
      p. cm.—(The misadventures of Peter Paul Pappenfuss)
  Summary: Mischievous fifth-grader Peter Paul Pappenfuss somehow
manages to become his parochial school's representative in a city-wide
academic contest, and in preparing, he learns more than facts and
figures.
  ISBN-13: 978-0-8163-2329-6 (pbk.)
  ISBN-10: 0-8163-2329-1 (pbk.)
  [1. Behavior. 2. Contests. 3. Church schools. 4. Schools. 5. Christian life.
6. Family life.] I. Title.
  PZ7.P61462Day 2009
  dc22
                                                                2008049393

09 10 11 12 13 • 5 4 3 2 1

DEDICATION

To elementary school teachers—especially the pretty one I married.

ACKNOWLEDGMENTS

A big fat Thank You to God for His graciousness toward me. Thank you to my family and friends for their support and for being good sounding boards. Thanks to Wichita Adventist Christian Academy and Minneapolis Christian [formerly Junior] Academy for providing the real-life material for me to build from. Thank you to teachers and principals who work with difficult students and to preachers' kids, who patiently endure the congregations and expectations they are sometimes stuck with.

I would like to appreciate sarcasm inspired by human stupidity. I would also be lost without products made from sugar that give quick energy for high-output writing sessions when one doesn't have much time. British sitcoms and the Internet are also good things. And where would we be, I ask you, without breath mints? Not to mention nature and the world. If there were no world, then we would simply float in space without oxygen, which would not be fun for very long, I assure you. Especially when we suffocate and freeze to death.

Pastors and parents, of which I am, I implore you to read this book with your kids. And when you do, make sure you invent different voices for all the characters and act out the exciting parts.

Facebook and MySpace, you have united the world in harmony and obnoxious spam and/or applications and causes no one wants to be a part of. Well done.

And to my former Wii and new Xbox 360, I give great credit for not completing writing projects sooner.

CONTENTS

"Yeah, and then—"

"And *then*?"

"Yes, and *then* while he was falling backward, he flailed his arms like a maniac, and because he sits in the back of the room by the shelf with the fishbowl on it—one of his arms smacked the shelf and catapulted the fishbowl—"

"Catapulted the fishbowl!" exclaimed Principal Purvis, sitting up straight.

"It flew several feet—because it's not very big—and it smashed on the floor by the door."

"Smashed? As in glass everywhere?" he demanded, rising out of his chair and looking excited.

"Not to mention the fish," I continued. "That's the worst part."

"What could be worse?" said Mr. Purvis, sitting back down wide-eyed.

"Well, when the bowl broke it sent Horowitz tumbling toward the door of the classroom."

"Who's *Horowitz*?"

"Our goldfish. Anyway, Tommy Sneldon—the biggest klutz in the world because he *never* pays attention to where he's going—was on his way back from the bathroom when he opened the door and *stepped* right on Horowitz!"

"Do you mean to tell me," said Principal Purvis raising his bushy eyebrows, "that there is dead fish smashed into the fibers of the new carpet that we installed at the beginning of the year?"

"Not quite, because as soon as Tommy stepped on Horowitz, he looked at his shoe—and threw up all over the place." Principal Purvis was back over at the watercooler, except this time he was splashing water on his face instead of drinking it.

"Oh! Oh, what a mess!" he groaned.

"Yeah," I continued, "especially when Naomi—who's always sick anyway—got a whiff of it and puked. And that caused two other kids to puke, too, in sort of a chain reaction. That is why Ms. Witherspoon had everyone go into Mr. Thompson's room with all the sixth-graders. She told us that way she could clean it up without anymore *interruptions*. Then she sent me down here. Actually, things are pretty bad back there," I chuckled. "I'm kind of glad to be here."

"Oh, that poor woman!" exclaimed Principal Purvis standing up. "And she's only a first-year teacher!" He put on his suit coat so fast he knocked over the stand it had been hanging on. Then he made his way out of the room, but not before whirling around and staring at me. "And as for you! You just wait in the office with Ms. Crabtree until I get back and decide a suitable punishment!" He opened the door of his office and raced out into the waiting area. His secretary looked up from her paperwork alarmed.

"Ms. Crabtree, don't let this boy out of your sight! Don't let him go to the bathroom, get a drink, or play with goldfish!" Then he bolted out of the office and down the hall.

Ms. Crabtree was a piece of work. She had the face of a bulldog and the personality of an enraged rhinoceros. She pointed an accusing finger at me and then pointed sharply to one of the office chairs. She didn't say a word, but watched me like a hawk eyeing a field mouse as I took my seat.

I plopped down and put my head in my hands and rubbed my temples. I was getting a headache. There was no telling how long I was going to be here. Rumor was that once a kid got sent down here on the last day of school, and Ms. Crabtree didn't let him go home but made him sit in the office *all summer*! Sitting in the principal's office is dangerous business.

The other bad part about sitting in the office is that it gives you time to think about the inevitable punishment you will receive when the principal comes back. I prefer to get my punishments right away—quick and painless. Instead, I was stuck here thinking about all kinds of bad things that could happen to me, while Ms. Crabtree periodically poked her bulldog face over her desk and glared at me. Whatever Principal Purvis ended up doing to me, I had to make sure the news didn't get home to my folks—which should be easy—as long as my sister, Mary, didn't find out.

Mary is in the third grade, always wears her blond hair in pigtails, and *never* makes mistakes. Never. She gets perfect grades, has perfect manners, a perfect knowledge of the Bible—even perfect teeth. She never gets in trouble at home or at school. For years, I've tried to tell my parents that she is abnormal and quite possibly an alien from outer space sent to study humans before the rest of her people invade earth and steal our water supply—but they don't listen to me.

The worst part about Mary is that she always has a way of getting me into trouble or making me look dumb—and I never see it coming until it's too late. She's sneaky. And when she does it, no one ever accuses her of tattling or being obnoxious. It drives me crazy.

I sat in the principal's office feeling relatively hopeful about my situation until I heard the bell ring and saw a bunch of little kids walking down the hall, past the door, coming from recess. There were kindergartners . . . first-graders . . . second-graders . . . oh, no! Third-graders—*Mary's class*! I needed to hide. I couldn't risk Ms. Crabtree getting a hold of me, and I couldn't crawl into the hallway—I'd be spotted for sure.

I noticed some magazines on a table by my chair, so I quickly grabbed one and held it over my face.

"Peter?"

Oh, great!

"Peter!" Ms. Crabtree's voice boomed out. "I believe Mr. Purvis said you were to sit still and wait for him. No reading. Peter, put that magazine down this instant!" It was useless.

I slowly closed the magazine and turned to put it away, only to find Mary standing in the doorway staring back at me. She had two bright blond pig-tails, her brand-new red dress on, and was grinning from ear to ear. Then she turned around and got back in line.

CHAPTER TWO
THE WALK OF SHAME

It was a long walk back to class. Shortly after Mary spied me, Principal Purvis came back and informed me that the class was ready to have me back if I could behave myself, but I would be receiving two weeks detention and a note to show my parents. Two weeks of sitting in Ms. Crabtree's domain doing nothing but homework! No recess. No eating with anybody. And no fun.

I walked down the hall as slowly as possible. I always hate this part. Whenever you get in trouble, you have to take the "walk of shame"—from the principal's office, down the hall to your class, and then to your desk. The classroom door is *always* shut, so you *have* to knock. This, of course, alerts everybody to your presence.

So when the teacher eventually answers the door—and I say "eventually" because she never answers on the first knock—you have disrupted class. The entire room stares at you like you have three heads as you walk to your desk. And everyone keeps staring at you even when you sit down.

Then, after the teacher gives you a minilecture or makes you give a public apology, you have to endure the questioning. Millions of questions whispered at you from every direction—like nobody knows what happened. It's so irritating. I hoped today would be different.

I stood outside the class door for about five minutes before peeking in through the little window to see what people were doing. There they were.

The "Unlucky 13" . . . or "11" right now, because I was out in the hall, and Lucas Snodgrass—the smartest kid in class—was sick today. We got our name—the "Unlucky 13"—because up until this year, there have been at least twenty kids in the fifth-grade class. When the school board found out enrollment was to be low and that there would be only thirteen students in our class, someone made a joke, saying it was an unlucky sign.

Word of this joke leaked out in the form of Billy Smith—the school board chairman's son. He told everyone about it at lunch the first day of school. The fifth-graders not only thought it was funny, but an invitation to embrace it as our class philosophy. Since then, half the class has had detention, and the other half hasn't been caught. We have had lectures on our behavior from our teacher, the principal, the school board chairman, and even the janitor; they all keep telling us that we are *not* the Unlucky 13. But it hasn't done any good.

My class is an odd mix. First, there are the guys: Tommy Sneldon (the klutz), Sam Feltzer (a kid who can't sit still to save his life), Lucas Snodgrass (the only kid who gets straight A's and whose head has a natural attraction to dodgeballs), "Big Calvin" (a kid who eats more then the rest of the class combined and who can throw a ball so fast it breaks the sound barrier), Harley O'Brien (my best friend, even though he can't shut up), Wesley Crabtree (Ms. Crabtree's nephew and the biggest whiner in the Western hemisphere), and myself of course.

As for the girls, there is Naomi Watson (a girl who is so easily nauseated she can puke on command), Melissa Samford (who is so obsessed with horses that pictures of them decorate every personal belonging she has), Lacey Cromwell (a future fashion designer and critic of what everyone wears), Gretchen Schwartz (who has her own laptop and is known as the Walking Wikipedia), Jennifer Langley (a tomboy who is second in sports only to Big Calvin), and finally Chandra Peterson (who is so obsessed with cleanliness she scrubs her desk hourly with her own cleaning products that she brings from home). Like I said, we're an odd class.

I took a deep breath and knocked on the door. Ms. Witherspoon paused, but then started up teaching again. She is petite, has auburn hair, and would be considered pretty—if she weren't a teacher. I groaned and knocked again.

This time I heard a voice tell Ms. Witherspoon that someone was at the door. I heard footsteps and then heard the lock pop as the handle was turned. The door opened to reveal my teacher. Her hazel eyes scrutinized me for a moment before she spoke.

"Come in, Peter Paul. Take your seat." She was feeling merciful today and spared me a lecture or public apology, but everybody stared at me as I walked to my desk in the back of the room. Our classroom still had a summer theme, which only served to taunt us, because the fact that we are in this wretched building meant that summer was over. I walked to my desk, past some hanging suns wearing shades and the bulletin board featuring a swimming scene. Then I sat down quietly and exhaled, while one by one, each pair of eyeballs went back to looking at the teacher. Except for Harley.

"Where have you been? Have you been in the principal's office this whole time? Did you get in trouble?"

"No, stupid, I was in the bathroom for the past two hours trying to find the toilet paper—what do you think?" Harley laughed quietly to himself, but not quietly enough. Harley's never quiet enough. Ms. Witherspoon looked at us until he stopped laughing and the class went silent. I hate it when teachers do that.

"Thank you," said Ms. Witherspoon, wearing absolutely no expression. Then she smiled again and held up a stack of papers.

"He brought up the plane incident at Oshkosh," I whispered.

Harley's eyes grew big. "The Camporee of Doom? But that wasn't your fault!"

A cold stare from Ms. Witherspoon silenced our conversation. After a long, awkward moment, she finally spoke. "As I was telling the class just before you arrived, Peter, we have a wonderful opportunity to represent our school in the community." A collective groan arose from the class.

"Do we *have* to rake leaves for old people again?" moaned Wesley. This sent a wave of sniggering through the class, and Ms. Witherspoon once again employed the silent stare method to put an end to our glee.

"No, we are not going to rake leaves, Wesley, and I would prefer it if you referred to them as the 'elderly' and not 'old people.'"

Another hand shot up; this time it was from Tommy. "Is there going to be food?"

"Gross!" said Naomi. "How can you possibly think of asking a question like that after what you did, Puke-a-saurus rex?"

Ms. Witherspoon cut her off. "Alright, alright, that's enough, Naomi. We all feel bad about what happened this morning, but it's over, and we don't need to talk about it anymore." Easy for her to say. She wasn't the one in trouble and didn't have a sister who was going to tell her parents. "To answer your question, Tommy, I will say this. If this class does well in representing us, we will have a pizza party with ice cream for dessert—how does that sound?"

A cheer resounded through the room, which involved clapping, stomping, hollering, and Sam Feltzer—the class spaz—climbing atop his desk and doing a dance. It took Ms. Witherspoon five minutes to get Sam down, and I thought I heard her mumble something about talking to his parents about how much dessert they packed in his lunchbox.

The excitement was further dampened when Chandra asked the inevitable question. "So what *are* we doing?"

"I'm glad you asked. Class, we have been invited to take part in an opportunity to represent our school in an academic contest involving local Christian fifth-grade classrooms in Davenport. It is being sponsored by local Christian businessmen, who have graciously agreed not only to host this event at the Radisson Hotel downtown, but also to provide the prize money of ten thousand dollars, which will be donated to the winner's school! What do you think of that?"

"Is this going to affect our grades?" I asked. Ms. Witherspoon groaned and massaged her head.

"No, Peter, when you take this test and fail it, your grade will not be affected. And neither will the winner's grade no matter how he or she does at the contest."

Normally, I would be offended by a comment like that. But the fact of the matter is that I *was* going to fail the test. I didn't care. I didn't need anymore stress that day—after all, I still had to contend with my family after school.

Now, I'm not a bad student. I'm just the type of guy who embraces "average." I figure that way I won't get stressed out, and I'll still get to go to the sixth grade next year. Besides, Lucas gets straight A's all the time and still gets pummeled in dodgeball. At recess, he is always picked last for teams. A's aren't much help when a rubber ball is flying toward your head at a gazillion miles per hour. The way I see it, the number of times you get beaned with a ball at recess is in direct proportion to how many A's you get on your report card.

"Alright, class," Ms. Witherspoon commanded, "take out a pencil. We are going to take the qualifying test for the contest now. Make sure you have nothing but your pencil on your desk. You will have twenty minutes to take the test, and there are twenty questions."

Ms. Witherspoon walked from desk to desk, handing out the dreaded quiz. I could see some kids who cared a little, looking deep in thought. Others looked confused. Me? I felt no worries. I didn't care. So, one by one, I circled my answers without even reading the questions at all. I marked a few A's, a couple of B's, several C's, and one D for "all of the above." The whole test took me only three minutes. Then I cleared off my desk, got up, and handed my test to the teacher.

"Done so soon, Peter Paul?" she asked sarcastically.

I nodded. "Absolutely."

"The bell isn't going to ring for another fifteen minutes, Peter."

"I know, but I've had enough for one day." She blinked and looked incredulous. But it was the truth.

She sighed and shook her head. "Go ahead, Peter Paul—just stay quiet for those who are still taking the test."

I nodded and went back to my desk and sat down. I got a few stares, but it didn't matter. I needed that last fifteen minutes to figure out just what on earth I was going to do when my sister told my parents about what I had done.

CHAPTER THREE
HOME

For some reason, Mary didn't say a word about the fishbowl incident as we rode home in the station wagon. Instead, she talked about the usual dumb stuff—grades, art projects, and her silly friends, Claudia and Chloe. I had warned Mom that the fact that Mary could make friends only with people whose names started with the letter *C* was a bad omen—a sign that something was wrong with her social development—but Mom said it was just a coincidence.

The majority of the time in the car I spent with my mouth shut, letting Mary take up Mom's attention. I just stared out the window at the telephone poles passing by—hoping that Mom would leave me in peace. However, moms can't leave you in peace; it's against their nature. So after Mary finished her talk on the importance of coloring within the lines during art, Mom turned, stroked my hair, and spoke.

"So, what did you do today, Peter?" I almost jumped when I heard the question, but it's of the utmost importance to stay calm in these situations—one voice crack, and you will give away your position.

"Not much. What did *you* do today?" I asked, looking back at her with the sweetest smile I had. She smiled back.

"Oh, not much. I just ran some errands."

"What kind of errands? Did you go to the grocery store?" I continued asking questions like this until we pulled into our driveway at 28 Oakbrook

Circle. Sure, it was a little sneaky, but I couldn't let her ask me any more about my day. If she did, I would be forced to skirt around the fishbowl incident, which would give Mary the chance to point out that I was forgetting something—and she would point it out.

Our house was located in Peaceful Glens—a new subdivision that boasted large backyards, a community pool, and walking trails. It was advertised as "A Community for the Sophisticated Family." My parents felt we all could use some sophistication, so we had moved in over the summer. We don't have the biggest house on the block, but it is a nice two-level house with four bedrooms, a finished basement, and a trampoline in the backyard.

I got out of the car and made my way quickly to the house. The lawn was freshly mowed, and the smell of grass was thick in the August heat. For the most part, the neighborhood was quiet except for a couple of kids riding their tricycles down the sidewalk. I went for the doorknob, only to find it locked.

"Peter?" Mom called out from the car. "Peter, why are you in such a hurry? Please come help us take some of the groceries out of the trunk!" I groaned and set my backpack down on the porch and went back to help.

"Honestly, Peter, do you really think your sister and I can carry all these by ourselves?"

"I, uh, have to go to the bathroom real bad."

Mary raised an eyebrow. "Interesting," she said. "You should really try to go before you get in the car, Peter. It's not good for your bladder—is it, Mommy?"

Mom shook her head. "No, it isn't, sweetie, and that's a very good point to remember."

I scowled at my sister—and she smiled back. I could see the little wheels in her head turning, and it made my blood boil. She bounced by me on her way to the house with her pink Hello Kitty backpack and one small bag of groceries—but not before she sang out: "I can't wait for dinner, Peter—can you?" She winked.

What is that supposed to mean?

"Uh, of course I can't wait," I said, trying to keep my cool, "I'm looking forward to it. What are we having, Mom?"

And then I remembered what night it was—Thursday. Health food experiment night! My mother is a nutritionist, and every Thursday she lets her zeal for health outweigh her common sense, and we are all subjected to a night of experimental cuisine. Health food experiment night results in a lot of leftovers.

Dad once told us that Mom used to cook like this all the time, but after three days of me not eating when I was in the first grade, the decision was made to have a "health night" only once a week in which Mom could experiment on us. Occasionally, she came up with a great recipe, and we heaped praises on it, hoping she would discontinue Thursday "health night." But we found that it just encouraged her. So every Thursday, we hold our noses and pray for mercy.

"Tonight we are having mango-squash soup with fresh rolls and banana-flavored tofu ice cream," Mom announced happily.

"I'm cool with the rolls, Mom, but are you sure it's natural for mangoes and squash to go together?"

"Sure, honey," she said, fumbling for her house key to unlock the door. "I saw it on television."

"But aren't *you* the one who tells me not to believe everything on television?"

She shot me a look that told me dinner wasn't up for discussion, so I tried for dessert.

"Could I have real ice cream?"

"No, Peter!" said Mom, unlocking the door. "We are all going to eat together, and we are all going to eat the same thing. I'm not running a buffet. Now, please take these groceries inside and get started on your homework."

I grumbled to myself as I set the groceries on the counter and then made my way upstairs to my room. I reached into my pocket and pulled out a nail. The doorknob on my door has a lock on the inside, and a simple round hole on the outside. So when the doorknob locks, you have to open it by putting a nail—the only thing that fits right—into the hole and pushing the lock which pops out the button on the other side. Technically, I'm not supposed to leave my room locked, but I do it anyway for one very important reason.

Candy.

Whenever a major holiday rolls around—like Easter, Christmas, or even Halloween—there is always an abundance of candy, whether it's in a stocking, a plastic egg, or a bowl for trick-or-treaters. At these times, I carry as much candy as I can get away with back to my room and hide it in a cedar chest my dad made me when I was little. The chest sits under my bed and has an old lock on it that I found in the garage. Technically, I'm not supposed to have candy or a locked chest either—and one year I got caught and my parents hid the chest for six months. But I got it back.

POP!

The lock was open.

"Peter! You're not supposed to be locking your door. It's rude!" It was Mary, standing behind me with her hands on her hips. She startled me so badly, I nearly poked myself with the nail.

"Well, you're not supposed to be judging people," I responded. "It's in Matthew chapter five or three or . . ."

"It's Matthew chapter seven, verse one," Mary said. " ' "Judge not, that you be not judged." ' "

"Exactly—you should know better," I said as I opened my door, went in, and shut it in her face—and locked it. *That little creep makes me so angry I could smack her.* But now was not the time. The important thing now was a little dietary supplement.

I threw my backpack on my bed and knelt on the floor beside it. I moved aside some strategically placed sneakers, a box of Matchbox cars, and a heap of dirty clothes to reveal my treasure chest. It was lying on its side, and I crawled halfway under the bed to grab it and pull it out. It was much lighter than it had been the last time.

I opened the lock and pulled back the lid to reveal what I had feared. My stash of candy was more than half gone. But there were still enough Snickers bars, Reese's Peanut Butter Cups, and Skittles to get me through supper. The chest held all sorts of other important stuff—my pocketknife with the bone handle, a pouch of coins I got when my family went to Jerusalem last year for my dad's ministers' meetings, and my prized possession, a little white box that held something my grandpa gave me before he died. But I'll never tell anyone what it is—not even you.

I crammed my face full of as much chocolate as I could in five minutes and then quickly hid the chest back under the bed before the inevitable happened.

There was a knock on the door. "Peter? It's Mom. Why is this door locked?"

"Because I'm naked!" I shouted, trying to sound panicked.

"Well, Mary said it was locked *before* you went in to get changed."

"Mary is an alien who is after my secrets and wants any excuse to come into my room!" I hoped Mom wasn't in the mood to argue and that my alien accusation would change the subject.

"Peter Paul Pappenfuss, I have told you not to call your sister an alien! It's extremely rude when all she is trying to do is the right thing."

"Sorry," I called out.

"Peter, I'm in no mood for sarcasm, either. Now get dressed and do at least thirty minutes of homework before your dad gets home. He just called and will be home in a few minutes."

"He's probably getting a burrito at Taco Bell," I said. "Can you call him back and tell him to get me one?"

"Peter, I don't care if you are not dressed—so help me I will come in there and make you appreciate the food you have if you do not stop pushing my buttons! Then I'll send your father in for a 'pastoral visit' when he gets home. Get dressed, unlock this door, and get to work!"

Once her footsteps faced down the stairs, I re-hid my treasure chest and sat on my bed. I have a Transformers bedspread with Optimus Prime battling the evil Decepticons on it. *I bet Optimus Prime doesn't have to do homework,* I thought. I grabbed my backpack, opened it, and laid out my books. I had four subjects that required attention. English (which I hate). Math (which I hate more). Reading (which I don't hate as much as English). And Bible (which I'm not sure if I hate or not).

I decided to start with Bible and flipped my Bible open to the book of Daniel. I got my Bible when I was little, and it has all kinds of babyish pictures in it. I try to hide them when I have to read in class, because it's embarrassing. We are reading the story of the fiery furnace in chapter three of Daniel. I've read it before. It was interesting the first time those three guys got thrown into the fire and God saved them, but now it takes every scrap of willpower to get through. I read a few verses, stumbling through the weird names, and stopped at the part where the king heats the fire seven times hotter. I flopped back on my pillow.

This is so boring!

I sometimes wonder what good it really does to read the Bible. How does reading the Bible help me put up with angry teachers, Thursday night health food, or an alien sister who never does anything wrong? It's not like I don't love God; I just don't feel very close to Him sometimes. He seems far away. If He is holding the universe together, helping all the people fighting wars and dying of cancer, why would He be concerned with a fifth-grader who can't even remember his memory verses?

Just then I heard the front door shut and my dad's voice calling, "I'm home!" I heard Mary running down the hall and down the stairs to greet him, and I started making my way downstairs too. My dad is a great guy, and I wish I could see him more. He has only one church to pastor, but it has three hundred members, and they call him for everything. They call him if the church alarm goes off, if someone is sick, if someone has an idea, if no one has an idea, and if they think he forgot to mention something that he should have mentioned in his sermon. Sometimes I wonder how church people survived before there were pastors to do everything for them.

I ran down the stairs to meet my dad. He was dressed in khakis, a brown sport coat, and blue shirt, holding a plastic bag from Wal-Mart and taking his dress shoes off. I gave him a big bear hug.

"Whoa there, sport! You nearly knocked me over." He gave me a squeeze. "How was your day?"

"Great!" I lied unconsciously, caught up in the excitement of seeing him. Mary gave me a look, and I glared a warning at her. She shrugged, winked at me, and went into the kitchen to help Mom.

"So what's in the bag?" I asked.

Dad smiled and shook his head.

"It's a surprise for later—after dinner. Is dinner ready, honey?"

"In about ten minutes. Why don't you get washed up while Peter and Mary help me set the table?"

Mary went straight to work setting out the silverware, and I lagged be-hind as I collected the plates. Mom was stirring the piping hot soup. It smelled strange. As we set the table, Mary looked up at me and smiled sweetly. This time I raised my eyebrows.

"What are you smiling at?" I asked. She smiled wider.

"Mom, can I say the blessing for supper tonight?" she asked.

"Of course you can, sweetie. Thank you for offering."

Mary finished setting the silverware and went to wash her hands. That girl was up to something. And I had five minutes before dinner to figure it out.

CHAPTER FOUR
MARY'S PRAYER

The dinner table looked great—except for the food. The big pot in the middle of the table was full of a steaming, orange liquid that made my stomach uneasy. There was also a pot of steamed Brussels sprouts that smelled and tasted like dirty feet. To wash it all down we each had a tall glass of tap water. I'm sure eating this way is healthful—if you can get it past your tongue and into your stomach without the taste killing you.

Once seated, we all joined hands. Dad glanced at the food and managed a weak smile before asking Mary to pray.

"Are you ready to have the blessing, sweetheart?"

"Yes, Daddy."

"OK then." We all bowed our heads, and my sister began to pray.

"Dear Lord, thank You for all the wonderful blessings You give us. Thank You for the great food that Mom has prepared. Thank You that we can all be here. Thank You for bringing us all together. Oh, and thank You for . . ." As Mary kept on thanking the Lord for everything He had done, is doing, and will do until the end of time, my mind drifted to Transformers, baseball, and what Mary's insidious plan might be. However, my brain snapped back to reality when she began bringing in her prayer for a landing.

"Finally, Lord, please help my brother Peter to repent of the evil he did today at school when he kicked Sam Felzter's chair over, which caused the goldfish bowl to smash on the carpet, sending the goldfish flopping toward the door only to be stepped on by Tommy Sneldon, which in turn caused him to puke all over the new carpet, inspiring others to do the same. Amen."

CHAPTER FIVE
MARY'S PRAYER ANSWERED

"Peter! Peter Paul Pappenfuss, you open your eyes right now!" demanded my mother.

"I'm praying."

"You most certainly are not praying!"

"I am, too!" I yelled. I was praying for the Second Coming to occur before they pried my eyes open.

"Peter. Look at me right now. Now!" Dad's voice was low, and he spoke very clearly, so I knew he meant business. Slowly I opened my eyes, unfolded my hands, and put them in my lap. I met Dad's gaze. His jawline was stiff. We looked at each other for a few moments. My face felt hot and uncomfortable. My palms were sweating, and for some reason, I was having trouble swallowing.

"Peter," said Mom, breaking the tension, "is there something you'd like to tell us?"

Of course there wasn't. What kind of a moron wants to tell his family about the trouble he got into at school? Why do grown-ups ask these idiotic questions? Meanwhile, the mood was growing tense around the table, and my mind was a total blank. With my parents glaring at me from either side, there was no way I could think clearly. Then there was Mary—the source of this horrible moment. She was adding to my blank slate by slurping Mom's mystery soup. She took long deliberate slurps that made my skin crawl. Then, she would pause after each slurp, look at me, and smile pleasantly before dipping her spoon again. *Sluuuuurp!*

"Peter," said Dad coolly, sliding his chair back as if to get up. "Your mother asked you a question. Tell us what happened today at school—now."

Sluuuuurp!

There was nothing else for it—I was going to get into trouble while my treacherous sister sipped her soup as though each spoonful was the taste of victory itself. That's when a brilliant thought struck me: *I was going to get into trouble anyway—why not do it in style?* Besides, Mary had it coming.

Sluuuuurp!

"You know," I said calmly, staring right at Mary and slouching just a little in my chair so my feet could reach. "It's hard to put what happened into words."

Sluuuuurp!

"Well, why don't you try, Son," said Dad, growing impatient.

Sluuuuurp!

"I've got a better idea," I said, smiling at my sister whose grin was beginning to be replaced with a look of concern as she continued with her soup.

Sluuuuurp!

"And what is that?" asked Mom.

"Well," I began, waiting for just the right moment, "since it's hard for me to describe, I figured it would be better if . . ."

Sluuuuurp!

"Yes?" asked my parents thoroughly agitated. I grinned wider at Mary as she bent over her soup bowl to take a sip—her new red dress dangerously close to the steaming orange goop. I made my move.

"If I showed you!" I cried and kicked the front legs of Mary's chair from underneath the table. The timing was perfect.

Mary's chair flew backward. Mary's head flew forward—right into her soup bowl!

* * * *

27

I had been in my room, lying on my bed for twenty minutes, before Dad knocked on the door.

"Can I come in, Peter?"

"Sure."

Dad slowly opened the door, stepped in, and shut it behind him. He had the bag with the surprise in his hand. He made his way over to the bed and sat down softly next to me. He didn't say anything.

"Did Mary enjoy her swim?"

"Peter, you know that isn't funny." Actually, I *did* think it was funny; it was everybody else who was suffering from a lack of humor. However, I was mad at Mary—not at my parents.

"Was there a big mess to clean up?" I asked, sitting up.

"The table, the floor, and a little bit of the ceiling were splattered with orange soup—not to mention Mary's new dress which Mom is laundering right now."

"So it was as bad as it looked?"

"Pretty much. Why did you do it, Pete?" I hated that question. Parents always ask that when you get in trouble, and the answer is always the same.

"I dunno."

"You don't know? You have no idea why you kicked your sister's chair and ruined her dress?" asked Dad, only slightly raising his voice.

"No!" I shot back. "I mean, I guess I was mad at Mary. Dad, she always finds some way to get me in trouble; she's deranged! Her biggest dream is making my life a nightmare and—"

"Was Mary the one who got you into trouble at school?" Dad interrupted. I paused trying to think of a comeback.

"No," I said eventually.

"So then, what was it that made you kick over Sam Felzter's chair?"

"I dunno."

"Did you think it was funny?"

"Only up until the fishbowl went flying through the air," I replied quietly.

"And what if Sam's head had struck the shelf, and he had been seriously hurt?"

Leave it to a parent to bring up the worst injury possible and suck the humor right out of a potentially great joke. Dad sighed and stood up, leaving the bag on the bed.

"Peter, I don't know why you have been having such a hard time this year. I don't know if it's because you're bored or because you are angry at us for something—"

"Dad! I'm not . . ."

"The only thing I do know, Peter, is that when you do things like this, it doesn't just affect you. I spoke with your principal after we sent you up here to your room, and we are going to have a meeting tonight. Just me, your principal, and a couple of school board members."

"What? But why? Why do you have to go in?"

"Because someone has to take responsibility for what you do, Peter. And as your parent, that job falls on me."

"But you're supposed to be *home* tonight!" I shouted, clenching my fists. I felt like hitting something. "We were going to practice football in the backyard tonight!"

"Well, Peter, you should have thought of that before you kicked Sam's chair. Now both our evening plans are altered, and I have to go." I could feel my throat tighten and my face get hot, and I fought the stinging tears in my eyes, holding them back until he left. I wanted to make things better and didn't know what to do.

"I'm sorry, Dad," I said, choking over the words just a little. He smiled at me and gave me a hug. He squeezed the tears right out of me, and I wiped them on his sport coat before we broke the embrace so he wouldn't see.

"I'm sorry, too, Son. I know you wanted to hang out tonight—and I did too. Maybe if I finish my sermon early tomorrow, we can do something together in the afternoon—OK?" I nodded. "In the meantime, you can enjoy what's in the bag."

"You're still going to let me have it?" Dad put a hand on my shoulder and gave it a squeeze.

"Peter, I don't buy you things because of what you do. I mean, sure it would have been nice to have celebrated a detention-free week—but ultimately, I give you things because I love you. I saw this on sale and knew you had wanted it for a while, so I got it for you. I hope you like it. Now then, I really need to go. Have a good night, Son." Dad left and shut the door behind him. I put my ear up against the door and listened to him tell Mom and Mary goodbye. Once I heard his car leave, I went back to my bed and stared at the bag.

Carefully I picked it up. It felt heavy, and I had a feeling I knew what it was. I slowly opened the bag and peered in. It was what I thought it was—and it made me feel terrible. I put my hand in the bag and lifted out a brand-new Optimus Prime action figure—the leader of the Transformers. It was worth a month's allowance, at least. The plastic package was huge, and Optimus was brightly colored and fully equipped with a huge laser cannon. I wanted to open it and read the booklet that comes with it that tells how to change Optimus into a semitruck and back again. But I couldn't.

I was struck with extreme guilt every time I went to pry open the plastic container that held Optimus in suspended animation. So I just stared at it for a few minutes. Then I read all the descriptions on the back of the package—all the fun I could be having with Optimus. Twice. It was no use. I couldn't shake the feeling. I got up and pulled out my treasure chest from under the bed. I cleared out a few more pieces of candy to soothe my soul and to make room. Then I gently placed Optimus in the chest, closed the lid, locked it, and returned it to its hiding place.

I lay back on the bed and thought about things. I didn't feel so bad about Mary and her dumb dress or even the stupid school carpet. But I did feel bad for my father. It wasn't fair that he had to go in for some dumb meeting that would be nothing more than a bunch of grumps bickering at my dad because they had nothing better to do. It wasn't like the carpet wouldn't have gotten stained eventually. I mean, how long could it last in a room where glue, paint, and glitter are used on a daily basis? They should thank me for breaking it in.

There was a knock on my door. It was Mom.

"Peter Paul? Honey, you can come out when you are ready to apologize to your sister."

"OK, Mom," I said absentmindedly.

"I'm sorry your father had to leave. I know how much you were looking forward to football. If you want, we could go outside, and you could throw it to me."

I had to suppress a laugh. I love my mom, but she throws like a drunk monkey. "Thanks, Mom. I'll be out in a few minutes."

"Alright, but don't stay in there all night."

"I won't."

I sat up and took a deep breath. Then I made a promise to myself and to God that I was going to change. I felt bad that what I had done had messed up everyone's evening. I also felt bad that my parents had to deal with so much stress because of what was going on at school. I wanted to make it up to them. So I asked God to forgive me, and then I promised that starting tomorrow morning, Peter Paul Pappenfuss would be so good and well behaved it would scare people. Then I went to apologize to my dumb sister.

CHAPTER SIX
THE NEW PETER PAUL PAPPENFUSS

"Does anyone know the answer? Peter, are you raising your hand again or have you just developed a nervous twitch?" My new approach to life was being met with mixed reviews. It was Friday, and I had volunteered to answer every single question Ms. Witherspoon asked. And although I had gotten only one answer correct so far out of the nineteen times I raised my hand, I still felt that it demonstrated to the class my serious commitment to change my life.

"Well, Peter?" said Ms. Witherspoon, tapping her foot. "If you know the answer, then come up to the board and write it down." I got up from my desk and made my way to the board. I picked up the black dry-erase marker and took off the cap, letting its pungent odor waft into my nostrils. That's probably why my mind went completely blank as I lifted the marker to the board.

"Um . . . ," I said, "let's see. If . . . ," and I began to mumble incoherently under my breath as if I were working out an answer, when in fact I was simply trying to remember the question. I could hear the occasional giggle from my classmates. *Come on, stupid brain! Remember!*

"Peter, are you alright?" asked Ms. Witherspoon.

"Couldn't be better!" I said brightly, which is another part of the new me. I am sarcastic by nature, and it gets me in trouble. So the new me is happy all the time—even if I don't feel happy.

"Maybe his batteries are low!" hollered Sam. Everyone sniggered. I had a few things I could have said about Sam's batteries, but instead I laughed it off and tried to focus on the answer. But it was no use.

"Uh . . . I'm just trying to remember how to spell it," I lied. More sniggering from the class.

Ms. Witherspoon exhaled in an annoyed way, and a voice belonging to Lucas Snodgrass called out from behind me, "N-I-N-E! As in 'There are NINE planets in the solar system.' Of course, you could just write the *number* if it would be easier for you."

The class roared, and my face burned red hot. I wrote "nine" on the board and sat down, feeling everyone's eyes on me. I didn't raise my hand the rest of the day.

* * * *

The weekend wasn't any better.

During Sabbath School, Harley and I usually sneak pieces of candy designated for those who know their memory verses. We figure if we are saved by grace and God is no respecter of persons, then it isn't fair that only those who spend their week memorizing texts should be rewarded. However, this time, instead of helping Harley, I told on him—right as his hand was in the middle of the bag of candy!

He went into shock at my telling on him, so Old Ms. Cracklestaff had time to whirl around from teaching the lesson and see his hand in the candy bag.

"Harley O'Brien, you little thief!" she exclaimed. Now Harley was in double shock because Ms. Cracklestaff is a strict disciplinarian. She *loves* to discipline. It's her hobby. And since she is retired and has nothing to do, she gets to spend all week thinking up new ways to torment the kids in her Junior Sabbath School class.

"Well, we know how to handle thieves around here, Mr. O'Brien. Since you love sweets so much, I'm going to give them to you—all of them." Harley smiled prematurely in his ignorance, forgetting who he was dealing with.

"Really? You mean it?" he said.

Ms. Cracklestaff nodded. "I do indeed," she said coolly. There was something wrong with the way she relished her words—and then we found out what it was. "You are going to eat that entire three-pound bag of candy, and you are going to eat it right now. For, you see, we are all going to watch you eat it until class is over—thirty minutes from now."

"I can't believe it! Are you serious?" cried Harley, ecstatic at his good fortune.

"I am. Now, if you're going to finish that bag, you had better get started."

Harley didn't need to be encouraged again; he began cramming jawbreakers, chocolate bars, Sweet Tarts, and licorice in his greedy mug—grinning and taunting all of us who weren't getting any.

There is a saying "Never take candy from strangers," and I suppose it is good advice. But perhaps an even better saying would be "Never accept a bag of candy from a retired Sabbath School teacher who appears to be rewarding you for your misbehavior." As the half hour came to a close, Harley began to look a little green.

"I . . . I don't think I want any more candy," he groaned.

Ms. Cracklestaff grinned wickedly. "You have three minutes left, Mr. O'Brien, and there is plenty more candy to be had—*so get to eating!*"

Harley gingerly unwrapped a bite-size Hershey bar and slowly put it into his mouth, which was stained red, blue, and yellow from the jawbreakers. He chewed it four or five times and swallowed. It turned out that bite-size bar was one bite too many. His eyes got big, and we all finally realized our teacher's gruesome plan.

"I've . . . got to . . . ," said Harley, but he didn't finish his sentence. He didn't need to. He didn't have time to. He staggered to his feet and ran haphazardly out of the room. While Harley was presumably upchucking two pounds of sugary goodness, Ms. Cracklestaff turned to us and said, "Now class, what have we learned today?"

* * * *

Harley didn't sit with me in church like he usually does, but it didn't matter. I had other plans. I marched right up to the front row as the church service was starting, grabbed the hymnal, and waited for the opening song. When it came, I sang so loud that the organist hit wrong chords a couple of times. And when Dad started preaching, I shouted things such as "Hallelujah!" "Preach it, brother!" and "AAAAAAMEN!"

My enthusiasm produced results—although not the ones I intended. Dad lost his place several times during the sermon, which made him go longer than usual, and some old guy sitting behind me said that if I was going to "holler and scream," I should go to the mothers' room with the rest of the babies.

* * * *

I regrouped over the weekend and tried out some new ideas Monday morning. It was my job that week to empty the pencil sharpener, so I did it every hour on the hour, whether there were pencil shavings or not. Things went well until stupid Chandra Peterson wouldn't let me empty the sharpener.

"Peter Paul, I'm in the middle of sharpening my pencil. You can wait!" she snapped as I tried to do my job.

"Pencil shavings wait for no one," I cried, pulling the cover off the pencil sharpener with all my might. The result was a dust cloud of shavings that flew into the air and caked themselves onto Chandra's face. She screamed and ran to clean them off with soap, water, more soap, more water, and half a bottle of lotion. Personally, I thought the shavings were an improvement on her looks, but Ms. Witherspoon fired me on the spot.

* * * *

The rest of the week followed in the same spirit. Tuesday I tried to be a gentleman and clear away the girls' trays after lunch. When I offered to take Naomi Watson's leftovers to the trash, she smiled warily and handed me her tray.

"Thanks, Peter," she murmured.

"Not at all, m'lady," I replied seriously—and then subsequently turned around and tripped over my own shoelaces. I flung the tray of food backward, all over Naomi and her friends. Naomi threw up—naturally—and the rest of the girls shunned me the remainder of the day. Well, except for Gretchen, who handed me her tray after seeing the spectacle.

"Tough break, Pete. Next time, double-knot your laces. I looked it up, and you are three times less likely to trip if you do."

Tuesday at recess I tried to be a humanitarian and pick all the kids who normally are chosen last for dodgeball. The result was an all-star team of idiots who couldn't catch or throw the ball if their lives depended on it. It was a massacre. It was like the surprise attack on Pearl Harbor. My team was pelted with so many balls, some of the kids actually began claiming they were "out" even if they weren't hit. They were terrified. One kid got knocked off his feet by an expertly thrown ball and was subsequently hit seven more times before he reached the ground—and we only play with four balls.

Wednesday I avoided recess, as several people now had personal vendettas against me. I told Ms. Witherspoon I craved intellectual stimulation and asked to sit in on the eighth-graders' science lab. The short version of what happened involves a chemical that made me sneeze after sniffing it and two eyebrows belonging to Sarah Hanson that are now missing—thanks to a strategically placed Bunsen burner.

By Thursday the only people who weren't mad at me were Harley, Big Calvin, and Tommy. But that all changed when, desperate to make a good impression, I left the line during a fire drill to make sure all the little kids in kindergarten had made it out safely. Unfortunately, they all *had* made it out safely by the time I went looking for them. So, while I was searching for them, Ms. Witherspoon went searching for me. This resulted in fifteen minutes of wasted time and our recess being cut in half.

Now it's Friday, and everybody is mad at me. I'm going to have to do something spectacular if I'm going to win back their confidences.

CHAPTER SEVEN
PIECE OF CAKE

As a rule, I am morally opposed to getting up early in the morning. However, desperate times call for desperate measures. So I'm up at 7:30 A.M. That's thirty minutes earlier than I usually get up and fifteen minutes before anyone else in my lazy family gets out of bed, so I have plenty of time to put the frosting on my peace offering. Or so I thought.

Mom and I started on it last night after Dad and Mary went to bed so they wouldn't eat any. Say what you will about Mom's "health food night," but the woman hasn't forgotten the value of pastries. The problem was that by the time I came up with the idea of baking a cake, we didn't have time to frost it. Mom told me I could do it this morning and left out a recipe for me. But when morning came, I couldn't find the stinking cocoa powder anywhere—not in the pantry, the fridge, or even in the freezer.

I didn't have much time to search. The bus would arrive in twenty minutes, and I was still in my pajamas. I'd heard of only one guy ever trying to go to school in his pajamas, and let's just say he's still going to counseling for what they did to him on the bus. The only other place the cocoa powder could be was in the garage on one of Mom's numerous "bulk food" shelves. Although why it would be there was beyond me. The items on those shelves are better suited to Dr. Frankenstein's laboratory than for making desserts for discerning fifth-graders.

The garage smelled like gasoline and old clothes, and my personal opinion was that any food kept in this environment wasn't fit for human consumption. Nevertheless, I opened the door and made my way to Mom's surplus of food items. There were big jars of red, yellow, and brown spices. Next to them were containers of herbs and beans, followed by an assortment of canned goods, the contents of which I had no clue whatsoever. Right next to the mystery cans, however, was a small brown box with a fine chocolate-colored powder. Bingo!

Snatching the box and dashing to the kitchen, I began making the icing for the cake. It took only ten minutes or so, and I wondered whether I had broken some world record for frosting production. Grabbing the cake out of the fridge, I began smearing on the rich, chocolaty goodness. But I was running out of time! It was only ten minutes until the bus arrived, and my parents couldn't afford to pay for counseling.

"What are you doing, Peter Paul?" It was Mary; she was dressed and tying her hair in a ponytail.

I thrust the bowl of frosting into her hands along with the spatula. "Make yourself useful."

* * * *

When I returned, ready for school, Mary was gently placing some aluminum foil over the freshly frosted cake. I was pleasantly surprised—amazed would be more accurate.

"Thanks," I said, picking up the pan.

"My pleasure," she said, smiling.

Something wasn't right. Our interactions are never this friendly. But there was no time for an investigation. We had a bus to catch, and I had my class's confidence to win back. And as long as I could keep the vultures on the bus away from the cake, the day should be full of sweet success.

* * * *

The morning passed agonizingly slowly. No one said a word to me except when Ms. Witherspoon called my name as she was handing back our most recent spelling test. I failed. Apparently, *acceptable* doesn't have an *x* in it after all—nor do a number of other words that sound like they should.

Five minutes before the lunch bell rang, I walked up to the teacher's desk and told Ms. Witherspoon I had brought a special treat for the class.

"What is it, Peter?" she asked suspiciously.

"A chocolate cake," I whispered.

My answer seemed to relieve her fears, and she dismissed me to fetch it from its hiding place in the cafeteria's kitchen. Upon my return to the classroom, I set the pan on her desk, and she led me to the front of the classroom where she made the announcement. "Class? Can I have your attention please?"

"What's he done now?" grumbled Lucas.

"Yeah," said Lacey, "what mistake has he made now—besides wearing those pants with *that* shirt?"

"Now that's enough, class. Peter hasn't done anything wrong. As a matter of fact, you will be pleased to know that he has brought us a special treat today—a chocolate cake!" There was a moment of stunned silence, then an outcry of jubilation.

"CHOCOLATE!" cried Sam, and once again took to his sugar-inspired dancing atop his desk. And once again, it took Ms. Witherspoon five minutes to calm him down.

"I know one boy who's getting a *very* small piece," she muttered to herself as she finished with Sam and dismissed the class to wash for lunch.

It didn't take long for the kids to gulp down their lunches and clear their desks in anticipation of the chocolate masterpiece I had brought. I had to admit, as I unveiled it from its aluminum foil, that Mary had done a good job. No edge of cake was left uncovered by the rich, creamy-looking frosting.

Ms. Witherspoon cut the cake into equal pieces, and I delivered a piece to each student in the room. Finally I sat down with my piece, and Ms. Witherspoon with hers. My redemption was at hand.

"Alright, class, what do we say to Peter?"

True to form, the class responded in a monotone, but not ungracious, "Thaaaank you, Peeeter Paaappenfuuuuss."

Satisfied, Ms. Witherspoon gave us the green light to begin cramming the cake into our mouths. I waited for a moment, as the sound of twelve plastic forks clacked against twelve plastic plates as each student picked up a utensil and thrust it into the moist dessert, carving out a gooey piece and placing it into their gullets. Any moment the sounds of satisfaction would saturate my ears, and I, Peter Paul Pappenfuss, would be a hero.

"AGGGH!" shrieked Naomi. "AGGGHHH—AHHHH!" She was getting louder. I immediately turned around to see what was going on—had she swallowed her fork or something?

Just then Melissa shouted, "WAH-WHADTH THIDTH?" Her mouth was wide open and full of cake. It was not a pretty sight. I felt panic swelling in my chest. It couldn't be the cake, could it?

The boys cried out next. "It's . . . it's . . . ," stuttered Big Calvin, too horrified to finish his sentence.

Sam Feltzer came to the rescue. "IT'S NOT CHOCOLATE! IT'S NOT CHOCOLAAAAAATE!" he yelled, standing to his feet and letting the cake fall out of his mouth onto his plate in revolting, globulous lumps. Then he started scraping at his tongue with his hands. "IDTH NODT COMAN ODTH! IDTH NODT COMAN ODTH!"

Chandra, who hadn't yet tasted her cake and who was compelled by her compulsion to clean, grabbed the water bottle off the dry-erase board to spray the remaining cake off Sam's tongue. But she missed and sprayed it in his eyes. "I'M BLIND!" he shouted, forgetting about the cake in his mouth—and the cake on his desk, which he knocked onto the floor.

The rest of the class made a mad dash to the drinking fountain with Ms. Witherspoon close behind to try and subdue the mob. They were elbowing each other and crying, "He's poisoned the frosting!" I felt in a daze. I couldn't believe this was happening. I looked at my piece of cake and gingerly put a little of the frosting on my finger and tasted it. I spit it out immediately, but the bitterness still clung to my taste buds.

"What is it?" I said to myself. Unfortunately, Lucas Snodgrass heard me on his way back from the drinking fountain and sauntered up to my desk.

"It's unsweetened carob, Pappenfuss. My mom keeps some in her pantry as well."

"I . . . I really thought it was cocoa, Lucas—you gotta believe me."

He laughed. "Sure, Peter, I believe you."

"You do?"

"Of course I do. You are the most well-behaved student in school, except for your weekly trips to the principal's office, setting people on fire in the science lab, making everyone miss recess, and of course, your exceptional grade point average. What was it last year? NEGATIVE FOUR POINT ZERO?" My blood was boiling, and I felt a strong urge to punch Lucas in the gut.

"Face it, Pappenfuss, you'd get into trouble even if you were trying to be good. You're hopeless. And next time, if you are going to mess up everyone's day, at least try to leave our lunch break alone."

I cocked my fist, ready to swing. But my rage was giving way to another emotion—one that made my eyes wet and burning. Shoving Lucas aside, I made my way out the door and ran. I kept running as Ms. Witherspoon called after me, "Peter! Peter! Come back here; I want to talk to you!" I didn't know where I was going, but I knew she wouldn't dare leave the Unlucky 13 unattended.

I managed to slip past a line of seventh-graders on their way back from gym class, which was good news because that meant the gym was empty, and there is a great place to hide under the stage area where all the gymnastics equipment is stored.

I crawled back past sweaty-smelling mats and pads into the darkest corner I could find. It only took five minutes before I heard voices looking for me. One of them belonged to Principal Purvis.

"Peter? Are you in here? Please come out; I'd like to talk to you about what happened."

Yeah right. There was *no way* I was going to talk to him. I could sense the anger in his voice. He called a few more times, then left. I waited for two more minutes, then let the tears fall. They rolled down my cheeks, burning all the way down. I curled up and hugged my knees to my chest. I felt so stupid. Stupid for having tried to be something I'm not. Stupid for having failed at even simple good deeds. Stupid for having run out of class to cry like a baby—and . . . *where was God?*

After all, none of this mess would have happened if I hadn't been trying to be a good Christian and help out my dad. He has enough troublemakers in the congregation without having his son being one. *God, why didn't You help me? I mean, aren't You SUPPOSED to help people do good?*

I spent the rest of the school day under the stage telling God how mad I was. And when I finally sneaked out and found Mom waiting for me out front in the car with my sister, I told God I had had enough. I was through trying to do good. It wasn't worth it.

"Peter, where have you been?" Mom demanded as I got into the car. "Everyone has been worried looking for you!" I shrugged and remained silent—feeling the tears threatening to come back.

"Peter, I spoke with Ms. Witherspoon already, and she gave me your things. I'm so sorry you had a bad day, but you can't just run off like this, honey. Now sit tight, and I'll be back. I have to let your teacher know that we've found you."

I lay my head back against the car seat and looked in the rearview mirror. I saw Mary sitting right behind me, coloring, with a smile on her face. My rage returned.

"Thanks for your help this morning, Mary," I said coolly.

"No problem, Peter. How did everyone like the cake *you* made them?"

I swallowed hard. "Oh, fine. They thought it was a scream." Mary fought to keep her smile from turning into a grin. My hand slowly drifted to the lever attached to the underside of my seat. "You know, I learned something today, Mary."

"And what was that, Peter?"

"That it never works out—trying to be something you're not." Her coloring slowed down just a little.

"What do you mean?"

"Well, it's like that picture you're coloring. You've put some time into it, I see. It looks nice."

She looked up mildly concerned. "Thanks."

"Don't mention it. But as I was saying, it's like you work so hard to paint a beautiful picture of something . . . ," my fingers wrapped tightly around the seat lever, "only to have it ruined by forces you can't possibly control or see coming."

She rested the point of her red crayon on the nose of the clown she was coloring and looked alarmed. "Peter, what are you doing?"

I sighed. "I don't know. Just talking. I've had a long day. Never mind me."

Just then Mom reappeared at the school entrance and was making her way to the car. Mary started coloring again and, for a moment, I waited, watching Mary carefully fill in the clown's nose with the bright red crayon. Then I pulled the seat lever, sending my chair flying back onto her lap.

It felt good to be me again.

CHAPTER EIGHT
THE CHOSEN ONE

After a week of failing at good behavior, it felt good to have a weekend when I could excel in more familiar territory.

Sabbath School saw my return to candy snatching. And although Harley was too distraught from the previous week's punishment to join me, he was pleased to see me back to my old self.

"Well, it's about time," he whispered as I was placing a handful of Smarties in my pocket while Ms. Cracklestaff's back was turned.

"Tell me about it," I whispered back. Just then we heard a knock on the door, and Ms. Cracklestaff lit right up and clapped her hands for joy.

"Oh excellent! Our special guest is here!" A collective groan softly made its way through the Junior room.

About a year ago, Ms. Cracklestaff had been campaigning for more help in the Junior division. She felt that she shouldn't always be the one up front teaching the kids. We heartily agreed. However, the only person willing to help was a retired guy named Harold Crosby.

Mr. Crosby is the type of grown-up who frowns even when he's smiling. And his sole purpose in life is to bore kids half to death with stories of all the "sins" he committed growing up and how if we don't watch out, we could end up making the same mistakes he made. But just in case that doesn't work, his stale breath and his thirty-year-old suits are enough to convince anybody that they don't want to do anything to end up like him.

Ms. Cracklestaff opened the door, and in slid Mr. Crosby. All around the room, students tried not to make eye contact and held their collective breath. He sauntered to the front wearing a classic pea-green, polyester ensemble and thick-framed glasses around his beady eyes. "Ms. Cracklestaff, I dare say we have a group of sleepyheads here this morning!" She nodded. Delighted that his observation seemed to be correct, he hoisted his pants higher and bent down to where he could almost look in our eyes. You could see him selecting the morning sin to be discussed.

He picked the sin of not eating a good breakfast.

That's the other bit about Harold Crosby. He thinks *anything* is a sin— or a lack of anything. I was always under the impression that sin has more to do with how we relate to God and each other, but being nitpicky about behavior apparently is more exciting to discuss. However, this morning, I was ready for him.

"I know you kids like to sleep in and barely make it to church on time and think you're awake enough to participate in the divine worship service. But I have news for you. You can't particiPATE if you aren't in the right psychological STATE."

"Amen!" I said loudly.

"Who said that?"

The class stayed silent, although there was a definite giggle suppression going on.

"Well, no matter. As I was saying, you can't function if you don't get up in time to feed your brain."

"Amen!" I agreed. Mr. Crosby couldn't figure out where the amens were coming from, so he kept going. Ms. Cracklestaff began to watch her class more closely to find the culprit. I was about to make a scene.

"I used to sleep in, too, and . . ."

"Amen!"

"Pappenfuss!" snapped Ms. Cracklestaff. "What on earth are you 'amening' for?" I didn't reply—only smiled. Her eyes narrowed. Seeing a possible standoff, Mr. Crosby decided to come to her rescue, which was exactly what I wanted.

"Oh, I see, Ms. Cracklestaff. We have a smart aleck among us." He made his way toward me and stood in front of my chair. When Ms. Cracklestaff tried to interject, he held up his hand. "Oh, I know how to handle the likes of smart alecks. Allow me." He unbuttoned his suit coat and knelt down in front of me. The class was riveted; they hadn't been this attentive in weeks. And they were grateful to me; I could feel it. So I continued.

"Do you think you are above breakfast, young man?"

I smiled.

"Well, let me tell you what happened to me when I didn't eat breakfast."

"Amen!"

Mr. Crosby's eye twitched a little before he continued. "I had to walk to school and never had the energy to walk fast enough to make it on time."

"Amen!"

"I arrived late, and my teacher slapped my wrists three times with a wooden ruler, and . . ."

"Amen!"

"It REALLY HURT and . . ."

"AMEN!"

Mr. Crosby was on his feet now, shouting. "AND I WISHED I HAD EATEN BREAKFAST!"

I stood as well and looked him in the eye. "AMEN!"

"WHAT ARE YOU 'AMENING' FOR!" cried Mr. Crosby at the climax of our discussion, causing several people to finally poke their heads into the room to see what was going on.

Ms. Cracklestaff was swift to administer justice. "Peter Paul Pappenfuss, go to your parents! I shall not allow you to make a mockery of Mr. Crosby's lecture!"

I grinned and nodded politely. I bent down and grabbed my Bible off my chair and whispered to Harley, "I'll see you in the lobby after Sabbath School. Enjoy your lecture."

Mr. Crosby was still fuming and slightly bewildered when I made my way past the onlookers in the hall to my parents' class.

* * * *

My parents were not pleased to see me arrive at their adult class, however, because they knew I had had a rotten week, they weren't too hard on me.

"Peter, I don't even want to know what you did to get sent here," said Dad, "but you will apologize to Ms. Cracklestaff before church."

I spent most of the church service in the lobby talking to Harley instead of listening in the first pew. There were always kids and several deacons who enjoyed milling around out in the lobby, so we didn't look conspicuous.

"So what happened after I left?" I asked.

"Oh, it was great," said Harley. "Mr. Crosby was so flustered by you saying 'amen' at all his negative points, that he spent the rest of the time talking about using words in their 'appropriate context.' Then he made the mistake of asking us if we could think of any inappropriate word choices. Well, since you were so bold, and since he asked, I volunteered a word I heard my uncle say last week. Everybody laughed, and a lot of other kids started volunteering inappropriate word choices. Ms. Cracklestaff ended up letting us out early. You truly have a gift for inspiring mischief, my friend."

"Thanks," I said smiling.

* * * *

I spent most of Sunday avoiding my homework, which meant I would have no way of humiliating myself by attempting to answer questions in class the coming week. I got up at 11:00 A.M., watched some cartoons, and went to Harley's house to play video games—since my parents won't let me have any. Harley has a Nintendo Wii, and I spent the better part of the afternoon schooling him in baseball. But he owned me in tennis.

Before I went to bed, Dad came to "tuck me in." I've told him repeatedly that I'm too old to need "tucking," but he insists.

"Hey, Pete, how was your day at Harley's?" Dad sat on the edge of the bed.

"Not bad. I still wish *we* had some video games."

Dad smiled. "It's not up for discussion, Peter. If we had them here, we'd all be mindless zombies, and we'd have to pry the controller out of your hands with a crowbar." I tried not to smile.

"Anyway, we want you and your sister to use your imaginations instead of having a computer imagining for you."

"Speaking of the runt," I said, "is it possible for her to miss out on dessert for the next week?"

Dad shook his head. "Peter, your mom already told me everything—including your request. We've talked with Mary, and she feels bad and is planning to apologize."

"Planning to apologize!" I cried. "Whenever I do something, I get locked up until I say 'I'm sorry.' How come she gets so much time to think it over?"

"You and your sister are different people, and the way we punish you wouldn't necessarily work on her."

"Yeah. You know, I wonder what it's like to have a no-punishment policy from your parents when you get in trouble."

"Peter, that's not fair. Mary is younger than you and doesn't get into situations as often as you do."

"That's because she's a criminal mastermind," I muttered to myself.

"What was that?"

"Nothing."

"Peter, I really want you to have a better week. I know last week was a big flop. Is there anything I can do to make things easier for you?"

"Pray for me," I said half serious, half sarcastic.

"I do—everyday, Peter. But I'll spend a little extra time this week."

"Thanks, Dad," I said, without sarcasm this time.

"Now, let's say our prayers and get to bed."

I lay back down under the Transformers covers, and Dad knelt by the bed. We closed our eyes, and Dad began to pray. "Dear Lord, thank You for how good You are to us—that we have food, shelter, clothes, and each other. I want to ask You to watch over Peter this week. You know he had a rough time last week and tries to do the right thing. Encourage him and provide him with ways to serve You that match his personality and strengths. Help him to find the role You've asked him to play in this life, and draw near to encourage him and help him along the way. Help us to know how we can be a blessing to him as well. In Jesus' name, Amen."

* * * *

Monday mornings are a curse. Not just because it's the beginning of another long week of trying to learn something at school, but because before Davenport Junior Christian Academy has classes, we have to endure one of the seven deadly plagues—more commonly known as chapel.

We all filter in to the multipurpose room and sit in our designated rows of ice-cold, folding steel chairs. Once we're all in and settled, Youth Pastor Joe—who is actually a Bible worker on half salary—springs to the front of the room and begins singing worship songs and exuberantly playing his guitar. He is happy as a lark, wandering the room and singing at top volume to seventy kids who wish they were still asleep.

What bothers me most is that if any one of us tried to do at home what Pastor Joe does, we'd all get in trouble. On Sundays I'm allowed to get up whenever I want—to watch TV or fix myself breakfast—under one stipulation: that I keep quiet. Once I laughed too loud, and my half-awake parents made me turn off my TV show and told me to go read in my room until they got up. I can't imagine what would happen if I grabbed Dad's guitar and paraded all over the house singing at the top of my lungs.

This morning, Youth Pastor Joe opened with several selections involving "actions." The only action I was taking this morning was staying in my chair. It took a good five minutes to warm those icy seats, and I wasn't standing to sing just so I could sit back down to warm things up again.

"Peter?" It was Ms. Witherspoon. "Can you participate with us this morning?"

"I could, but I don't want my rear end to freeze." Several kids giggled.

"Peter," she said in a tone cooler than my chair.

Fine.

I stood to my feet as the song "Father Abraham" started. However, when Youth Pastor Joe said, "right arm," I moved my left, and when he said, "left leg," I did my right. I also made several of the older kids laugh when I began turning around three verses before you were supposed to. I was also the last to sit down when the "action" songs ended.

"Peter, you can stop spinning now," said Ms. Witherspoon, visibly annoyed. I stopped and sat down beside my sniggering classmates. Youth Pastor Joe had a short prayer, and then Principal Purvis stood and walked to the small wooden podium up front.

"Thank you, Pastor Joe. Good morning, everybody."

"Gmorrran Prinpul Purvs . . . ," mumbled the half-awake student body.

"Before we have our message this morning, we have a special announcement to make. Ms. Witherspoon, could you come up here, please?" I wondered what this was all about. Our class didn't have anything planned.

Ms. Witherspoon walked briskly to the front, smiling, and took the podium. She was holding an unopened, sealed white envelope. "Thank you, Mr. Purvis, and good morning to you all." We responded with even less enthusiasm to the second "good morning" of chapel. "As Mr. Purvis mentioned," Ms. Witherspoon continued, "we have a special announcement for you this morning. Two weeks ago, our fifth-grade class participated in a little quiz put out by the local Christian Businessmen Association to see who will represent our school at an academic contest—and possibly win ten thousand dollars for our school!"

"When was this?" cried Lucas. Ms. Witherspoon tried to keep her cool at this outburst from her most academically inclined student.

"Two weeks ago, Lucas. I'm afraid you were sick that day." The visible shock and disappointment on Lucas's face made attending chapel worth the effort for several people who had grown tired of his snooty smartness—myself included.

"Tough break, Brainiac," said Big Calvin, clapping a semi-comforting hand on Lucas's shoulder. He recoiled.

"Keep your dumb mitts off of me, you cretin!" snapped Lucas, causing the older kids to roar with laughter. Calvin was about to turn his hand into a fist when Principal Purvis was on the scene.

"Boys!" he shouted. "I would very much like it if you would sit still and BE QUIET!" The students smiled, and the teachers looked surprised. Mr. Purvis corrected himself. "I mean, stop talking and pay attention." There was a soft snickering among the student body. Principal Purvis, turning red at the thought of being mocked, dismissed himself from the room, and Ms. Witherspoon, shaking her head, continued.

"As I was saying, we took this quiz to see who would represent our school in a contest for local fifth-graders. In this envelope, we have the results and the name of the winner!" A couple kids clapped; most yawned. Flustered, Ms. Witherspoon opened the envelope and held the letter to her chest, prolonging our lack of anticipation.

I leaned back in my chair. Harley had brought gum to chapel and was handing it out covertly. I swiftly popped a piece in my mouth. As I smacked and chewed, I whispered to Harley, "So, who do you think the poor sap is who gets to represent the school?"

He grinned. "Has to be the Walking Wikipedia—no one else carries that much useless information around, besides Lucas."

"Ha, whatever. Gretchen is cool. I was thinking it would be you; your grades aren't half bad."

Harley shook his head. "No way, man—I put all *b*'s on my test—there's no way I'm doing extra work for this establishment any more than I have to." I nodded my approval. Ms. Witherspoon took a deep breath; she was ready to read the results.

"I guessed on all my answers," I said to Harley's amusement. "That's why I finished in 'record time.' There's no way I'm doing extra work, either."

"You're a genius," replied Harley.

"I know. I . . ."

"And the winner is . . . is . . . PETER PAUL PAPPENFUSS?"

Ms. Witherspoon's shock was evident in her voice, and her eyes were the size of saucers. The students' surprise was evident in their silent stares. But no one was more surprised than I was. I lost my grip on the back of Harley's chair and went toppling backward—crashing into the sixth-graders behind me. To make matters worse, I swallowed my gum on the way down and began to choke.

It took a few moments for the surprise to wear off, so Mr. Talbot, the sixth-grade teacher, could run to my aid and whack me on the back hard enough for me to cough up a phlegm-ridden piece of Dentyne Ice Breakers gum at the feet of my fellow students. Harley laughed so hard I thought he was going to choke on his gum, and Naomi looked like she was going to be sick—along with several others. But what got my attention was Principal Purvis standing me to my feet with an exasperated and genuinely terrified expression. He had returned just in time to hear the results of the test.

"Peter! In my office. Now."

CHAPTER NINE
A Different Kind of Trouble

Like so many times before, I found myself in Principal Purvis's office, in the same hardwood chair, staring at disgruntled educators. Both Mr. Purvis and Ms. Witherspoon were on the other side of the principal's desk, carefully reviewing the contest rules, frantically looking for some loophole that would eliminate me and put someone like Lucas in the contest. They had been reading for twenty minutes, while the rest of the school was finishing chapel with Pastor Joe—who was asked to tell mission stories until they came back.

"Did you find anything yet?" I asked hopefully. They both looked at me expressionless. Principal Purvis spoke. "I don't know how you did it, but you have managed to get yourself into a completely different kind of trouble. How did you manage to get every question on this test right?"

I didn't answer. Who would believe that I got 100 percent out of dumb luck? Even I couldn't believe it. I had to admit that I was a little excited. Not because I would get to compete, but it was nice to have people in awe of my intelligence. However, most of me felt sick, nervous, and scared. It's one thing to fail a test in school, but if I competed, I was going to fail not only in front of my school but every Christian school in town. I let out a sigh.

Mr. Purvis did the same and sat down. "There's nothing for it, Ms. Witherspoon," he groaned. "He can't get out of this."

"I'm not sure what to say, sir," said Ms. Witherspoon. "It would be one thing if Peter wanted to participate, but judging by the green hue he has taken on in the last few minutes, my guess is he isn't thrilled about this either— are you?" I shook my head.

Mr. Purvis slid his chair to his watercooler and took a long drink. He crushed the paper cup and held it in his hand for a few minutes as he thought. "Peter, you've caused me enough grief this year. How I wish I could just give you detention and be done with it!" He got up and looked at the calendar on his wall. "When is the contest, Ms. Witherspoon?"

"October 22—one month from now."

"When did you say?" he said, suddenly seeming to have a new thought.

"Uh, October 22—Sunday afternoon and evening."

A weird smile spread across Principal Purvis's face.

"Well, Ms. Witherspoon," he began, turning around to face me, "if there is no way to prevent Peter from representing the school, then we will just have to make sure he does a good job!" He chuckled to himself. Ms. Witherspoon and I were too confused to speak, so Principal Purvis continued. He stood upright, hiked up his belt, and walked toward my chair, staring down at me.

"Pappenfuss, are you familiar with the 'Great Disappointment'?" I had heard something about it in Bible class and Sabbath School, but I couldn't recall just what it was at the moment.

"Not really."

Principal Purvis cleared his throat.

Oh great—a lecture!

"Back before our church officially organized, there was a man named William Miller who by studying the prophecies of Daniel and Revelation determined that Christ would come on October 22, 1844."

"Was he right?" I asked snidely.

Principal Purvis's eyes narrowed, but I thought I saw Ms. Witherspoon suppress a smile.

"Obviously not!" he retorted sharply. "But thousands of people believed Miller." Mr. Purvis stood up and paced toward his window, looking out at the parking lot and waxing eloquent.

"Miller's followers waited all that day and into the night, waiting for

Christ to come. And when He didn't, there was terrible grief. So great was their grief that in our church's history that date is called the 'Great Disappointment,' because what they had been hoping for never happened."

"Bummer," I said.

"Indeed," continued Mr. Purvis, turning around with the same strange smile. "But, later through Bible study and visions given to one of our church founders—"

"Ellen White?" I asked—purely guessing.

Mr. Purvis nodded. "The real meaning of October 22, 1844, was discovered. Despite Miller's mistake, God had led His people anyway." He laughed to himself at this point. I was starting to feel really nervous.

"Ms. Witherspoon," he whirled to look at her, at the same time pointing at me for emphasis, "how much detention has this boy received for his antics so far this year?" Ms. Witherspoon was standing in the corner of the room behind the principal with her arms crossed. She had been puzzling over his history lesson and shook her head to snap out of her trance.

"Uh, I believe two weeks, sir."

"Well, how about we make it six in light of this little stunt?"

"WHAT!" I exclaimed, shooting out of my chair. "You can't do that. I didn't do anything wrong. I . . ."

"MR. PAPPENFUSS!" shouted Principal Purvis so loud my ears rang. "You will never address me in such a manner, do you understand? Now—SIT DOWN!"

I stood frozen with rage, but Ms. Witherspoon sprang to my side before I did anything stupid. "Mr. Purvis!" she exclaimed. There was an icy, awkward moment between the two teachers. I slowly sat down without breathing.

After an eternity, Mr. Purvis broke the silence. "My apologies, Ms. Witherspoon," he said. Ms. Witherspoon placed a reassuring hand on my shoulder, as the principal unveiled his plan in much quieter tones. But somehow, I didn't feel any better after hearing it.

"Peter will be given four weeks more detention—*however*," he added quickly, before I could protest again, "it will not be spent in idle waiting or loitering or even helping to clean the classroom. It will be spent in rigorous study under the tutelage of our newest teacher, Ms. Maryann Wither-spoon!"

Now it was Ms. Witherspoon's turn to protest as I marveled at the revelation of my teacher's first name. "I don't have the time! I'm barely keeping up as it is," she wailed, "being new to this school and to teaching in general. I have papers to grade, bulletin boards to set up and tear down, and—"

"*And* tutor Peter Paul Pappenfuss so he doesn't embarrass the school!" Mr. Purvis straightened his tie and stepped very close to Ms. Witherspoon.

"Don't forget, my dear, that this contest was your idea in the first place. I went to bat for you at the school board meeting. I even signed that letter asking the contest committee to hold the competition on Sunday evening so our school could participate—and now you have the audacity to forsake the pupil who has placed himself in the contest on your behalf?"

Ms. Witherspoon swallowed hard, realizing there was no way out. "No, sir. I won't 'forsake' him. I'll . . . I'll do as you wish."

Principal Purvis smiled a smile that made neither of us feel happy. "Excellent! I'll call Pastor Pappenfuss and his wife to let them know the good news."

To my dismay, my parents *did* think it was good news. They were elated. And when they found out that the contest prize was ten thousand big ones, I could hear my dad shout "Whoo-hoo!" on the line—even across Principal Purvis's desk. After hanging up the phone, he told me my mother had said she would do anything to support my "tutoring sessions"—which in my opinion were worse than detention.

After that, Mr. Purvis dismissed Ms. Witherspoon and me—but not before placing a hand on my shoulder and giving it an uncomfortable squeeze, saying, "Let's hope that God will bless. And you know that the twenty-second was really the Great Anticipation, and it was the following day that was the real disappointment. Let's hope the anticipation on this year's October 22 won't end in a great disappointment." He walked us out of his office and sent us back to chapel where Pastor Joe would be running out of stories to tell. Then he shut his office door.

"Come on, Peter, let's go," said Maryann Witherspoon, and we walked— not saying a thing—back to chapel and the rest of the school day.

At the end of the day, an announcement was made over the intercom confirming to the entire student body that the school's reputation rested on my shoulders. My stomach bubbled and made noises when I heard it. Most people thought it was kind of funny; a few, like Harley and Gretchen, actually wished me well.

"You can do it, Pete," said Harley. "If you can *guess* a perfect score, just think what will happen when you study! You could be more than perfect!"

The only naysayer was Lucas, who approached me as I was putting my things away just before the bell rang.

"I heard that you will be competing on the day of the 'Great Disappointment.' How fitting. Try not to hurt yourself studying; don't want to burn out both your brain cells." Before I could pummel him, the bell rang, and he pranced away, laughing down the hall. Meanwhile, I was stuck at school for the next hour.

"Peter?" It was Ms. Witherspoon. She made her way through the stream of kids leaving to go home. "Are you OK?" I wasn't sure how to respond. I rarely took Lucas seriously, but I did feel ill. She motioned for me to sit down at my desk and took the desk next to me.

"This isn't what you thought or wanted to happen, is it?"

I shook my head.

She smiled. "Me either. I know you must feel a lot of pressure, and I do too. This is my first classroom, and I want to make a good impression. I thought this contest would be something simple, but it has gotten to be difficult. I also know that there are *some* people in this school that thrive on making life difficult for others." I wondered if she meant Lucas or the principal.

"In any case," she continued, "we have to work together, and we need to make the best of things. I promise I will try to make this fun and try to be energetic and helpful so the time passes quickly, but you'll have to help me—OK? And maybe, sometimes, I'll bring some snacks, and we can go outside and get some exercise. After all, physical education is still education, right?" She smiled warmly at me, and I felt a little better.

"Thanks, Ms. Witherspoon."

"You're welcome, Peter."

"Ms. Witherspoon?"

"Yes?"

"Could we start with physical education today?" She laughed—a genuine laugh, not one of those fake ones adults sometimes use when they want to make you think your jokes are funny.

"I think we can do that, Peter. I could use some fresh air. Would you like to take a walk?"

I nodded.

As we put our coats on, I asked Ms. Witherspoon if she thought I stood a chance to win.

"Do you mean do I think you have more than two brain cells?" I felt my mouth smile, even though I didn't want it to.

"Peter, I think you are as smart as anyone else your age—you just have to learn to apply those smarts to something other than mischief. And yes, I think you stand a chance at winning as well . . . if you're willing to work."

I hate work. But I hate the thought of looking stupid and proving Lucas right even more. So, for now, I'm at the mercy of God and my teacher.

CHAPTER TEN
THE BEGINNING OF HARD TIMES

"Tho whadh dthah goin dthoo, Peedtehr?" asked Harley with a mouthful of peanut butter and jelly sandwich, some of it sliding down his shirt.

"Harley, that's gross," scolded Chandra, who was sitting next to me across from Harley. "Why don't you chew your food before talking?"

Harley smiled, chewed his food delicately, then responded, "Why don't *you* sit somewhere else? You're going to give me indigestion."

Chandra made a face at him and then turned to me. "Ugh! Do you eat with him *every* week?"

Chandra wasn't the only new person having lunch with Harley and me. The entire class surrounded us as soon as we got to the cafeteria, and the kids in the other classes were very quiet at their tables so they could hear anything that was said. Only the sounds of chewing and slurping were heard.

"Yes, Chandra—every week," I replied. "And who cares, and why are you all so eager to eat with us?"

Chandra laughed a fake laugh. "Oh come on, Peter—as if you didn't know."

"Yeah, Peter Paul," chimed in Naomi. "There is only one reason I would brave your disgusting nature—and that reason happened yesterday." Everyone nodded and mumbled their approval. I had been afraid that was why they were eating with me.

"Which brings me back to my original question," said Harley. "What are you going to do?"

I took a bite of my sandwich, then took a long drink of milk, eyeing each of my classmates. I cleared my throat. "I'm going to do the only thing I can do," I said.

"What's that, Peter?" asked Gretchen, who was sitting next to Harley.

"FAIL!" said a poisonous voice from the far end of the table. It belonged to Lucas Snodgrass, who was glaring daggers at me. "The only thing Peter Paul Pappenfuss knows how to do is fail. Think about it. Who remembers Professor Pappenfuss from last week and all his learned answers?" A few people sniggered, which only encouraged Lucas.

"You hear people laughing, Peter? You'd better get used to it, 'cause when you mess up, it will be in front of a whole lot more people than this."

"Blow it out your ears, Snodgrass," snapped Harley. "You're just jealous."

Lucas narrowed his eyes. "Whatever," he replied sharply and stormed off to throw the remnants of his lunch away.

"He does have a point," said Big Calvin, who was sitting on the other side of Harley. "I mean you're *not* the best student in the class. How do you expect to compete?"

I sighed. "Well, for one thing—thanks to Principal Purvis—he's turned my detentions into tutoring sessions with Ms. Witherspoon." There was a collective groan of sympathy.

"Tough break," said Melissa, packing up her cowgirl lunchbox.

"Yeah, Pete, that's too bad," echoed Jennifer. "At least it's almost time for recess." This was true, and it offered me some comfort as I got up and took my lunch tray to the trash. As I turned around to go back to my seat, a large group of second-graders started chanting, "Peter's gonna faaaail; Peter's gonna faaaail!" And sitting quietly at the end of their table was Snodgrass, with a malicious grin on his face. Mr. Farnsworth, the second-grade teacher, managed to swiftly calm down his students. But the damage was done. Although most of my classmates sympathized with me, no one argued Lucas's point. They all thought I was going to fail, and apparently, so did the second-graders.

I was now angry *and* depressed, and not even recess was going to help.

No doubt this was what my life was going to be like until the end of this stupid contest. This was *not* worth ten thousand dollars.

* * * *

My second tutoring session began with Ms. Witherspoon pointing out that we had better start with my weakest area—math. I was afraid she'd say that. So for the next two hours—yes, you heard correctly, two stinking hours—I was subjected to torture that included timed worksheets, finding the multiples of various numbers, and playing a dumb game on the chalkboard called "find the missing number," which meant me staring at a long division problem that was missing a number, until Ms. Witherspoon finally gave up and told me the answer.

After I began developing a nervous tic after seeing so many numbers, Ms. Witherspoon changed pace a bit. "OK, Peter, I think we've both had enough numbers for one day. Why don't we move on to story problems? Something you may find a little more practical."

As soon as I looked at the first story problem—which had to do with somebody having apples and wanting to divide them among their friends, only to have one of their friend's friend cut up their apple and share it with more friends—I knew they weren't going to be practical. I sometimes wonder if anything in a textbook is. I managed to slug through five of them before Dad showed up to take me home.

"How'd it go today, sport?" asked Dad.

"I hate math," I muttered, picking up my backpack.

Ms. Witherspoon smiled and walked over to us. "Peter participated very well today. I think we're off to a good start."

"So, he's not as bad in math as he thinks he is, eh?"

I shook my head. "Dad, she said I *participated* well. She didn't say I *scored* well."

"Oh well, it's a start, right, Ms. Witherspoon?"

She smiled weakly. "That's right, Pastor—now about his homework—"

"I have to do *more*?" I couldn't believe it. Not only was my afternoon already used up, but this crazy woman was trying to snatch away my evening. "This is nuts! How am I supposed to have a normal life if all I do is homework?"

"Calm down, Peter; it isn't that much," soothed Ms. Witherspoon. "It will take only about thirty minutes. I think you'll live. And as soon as you start to understand how these math problems work, you can stop."

"Right," I snorted. "Until we begin a new subject."

"He'll do it," said Dad, putting a gentle, but firm, hand on my shoulder. "We're grateful for your help in getting Peter ready for this contest; it means a lot. I know being a new teacher is tough, and to have to do extra tutoring as well must be stressful."

"Thank you, Pastor Pappenfuss."

Dad nodded then tapped me on the shoulder. "Alright, Peter, let's go. There are a few moments of daylight left before supper, and I'll bet you could stretch those legs of yours a little. Football?"

I smiled. Football sounded good. However, I seriously wondered if running away and not coming back until after the contest would be a better way to stretch my legs.

* * * *

After a supper of macaroni and real cheese—for which I was grateful—I headed up to my room to work on math. As I climbed the stairs, I heard the phone ring and Mom answer it.

"Hello? Hi, Harley. Mmhmm . . . uh, huh . . . I see. Well, I'm sorry, Harley, but he has a lot of homework to do tonight. Yes, OK. Have fun!" Against my better judgment, I asked what Harley had wanted.

"Honey, I think you should just focus on your homework."

"So now I can't even *know* what I'm missing? Come on, Mom."

"Very well, the O'Briens are going to that little place on the west side of town with the go-carts, batting cages, and mini golf."

I felt sick and angry at the same time. "That sucks," I muttered. My word choice was not lost on my mother.

"Peter Paul Pappenfuss! I hope you didn't just say what I think you said; otherwise, you won't get to go anywhere even *after* the contest, do you understand?"

I grunted.

"Now, get up to your room, young man, and finish that homework—and *maybe* you'll have a little free time."

"Goodie," I said, "a little free time to brush my teeth and go the bathroom before bed."

I made my way to my room and sat at my desk with head in my hands. It wasn't long until her Royal Stupidness was standing in the doorway. All through supper, I had had to listen to Miss Perfect tell us about all the fun she and her dumb friends had after school at the playground in our neighborhood. Now, standing in my doorway—after she had monopolized the supper conversation telling us about all the sliding, swinging, and silliness she had participated in—she had the gall to ask, "So, what did *you* do after school today, Peter?" Little brat!

"What?" I snapped, without looking in her direction. She said nothing but walked over to my desk and peeked at my math assignment.

"Story problems?" she asked.

"Yeah," I replied, "and if you ask me, the real problem has nothing to do with numbers. The problem is that they are stupid stories. I don't give a baboon's elbow how many sugarplums Sally bought at Carl's Bakery or which one of her blockhead friends she gave the most to. I mean, if I was supposed to find out which sugarplum caused the fatal food poisoning of Sally's friends, then that might be a little more interesting."

Mary nodded. "I see," she sighed. "You know, Peter, I think this situation requires prayer." She bowed her head as I sat at my desk stunned. *Was she really going to pray for me? Did she feel bad at all? Did she care?*

"Dear Lord," she began, "You know what we're all going through, and You know Peter isn't the best student. I just pray that our school won't look dumb no matter how *bad* Peter does. Our school isn't as big as some, and so this is really important, because we can't afford embarrassment . . ."

And on she went. *How am I supposed to study with her going on like this?* I looked at my heavy math textbook. It probably cost a lot of money and was intended for someone to make use of it. And since I couldn't concentrate with that little imp praying about my inevitable failure, I closed the book. Just before she said "Amen," while her eyes were still closed, I whacked her with it!

* * * *

I spent the next thirty minutes in time-out while Mom iced Mary's forehead. Time-out consists of sitting on a kitchen stool while facing a corner located in the kitchen. It's not the most exciting time in the world—but at least I got out of half an hour of math. However, as I contemplated what I felt was a justified act of violence, I realized that this was only day two of my academic training and that I was already starting to crack. *This is going to be a lot harder than I thought.* I told myself. *And I bet somewhere, in some dark, dank place, Principal Purvis is laughing.*

CHAPTER ELEVEN

WORN-OUT

Officially, it has been two weeks since I started my after-school tutoring sessions with Ms. Witherspoon—and things aren't getting any better. It's not that I've gotten dumber, mind you; it's just that this whole mess has consumed my life. Even good things turn to ashes in my hands.

For example, Mom and Dad (despite generously giving me time-outs for any act of violence or any act that could be remotely perceived to have an intent of violence toward my sister) have noticed that my life is becoming forfeit. So, last Friday night, before family worship, they called me into the living room and gave me a present.

It was small in size, wrapped in metallic blue paper with a yellow bow. I could tell Mom wrapped it, because when Dad wraps gifts, they look like they've been put through the garbage disposal. I thanked them and tore into the package—IT WAS AN IPOD VIDEO!

My excitement was short lived, however, when my doting parents informed me that they had already programmed several educational MP3s onto it—thanks to Ms. Witherspoon. Mom showed me several "fun" songs about geography, the presidents of the United States, and memory verses my dad had recorded himself using the microphone in his laptop. There were even documentaries from the Discovery Channel about whales, outer space, and the environment . . . *my favorites*!

"Well, whaddya think, Pete?"

"Can I put some other stuff on this?" I asked pleadingly.

"Like what?" asked Mom.

"Games, *normal* music, or maybe a movie? Like *Transformers*?"

"We can talk about that after the contest, Peter," said Mom, a little annoyed at my ingratitude. "But for now, this is a tool to help you do well. Listen to it when you ride in the car, just before bed, or—"

"I'll just leave it on *all* the time. I don't have a life anyway, so it's not like I would miss anything."

"Peter, this cost a lot of money; don't be ungrateful," scolded Dad.

"Why?" I asked. "Will you take it back?" I don't think it was so much the question that got me sent to my room as the hopeful smile I was wearing when I asked it.

* * * *

I spent the weekend "being grateful" by listening to my iPod instead of playing baseball with the neighborhood kids or watching television. The only upswing was when I snuck the iPod into Sabbath School and watched my whale documentary instead of listening to Ms. Cracklestaff's lecture on the evils of television. I tried to keep it hidden, but at some point, I began noticing the uncanny resemblance between narwhals and Ms. Cracklestaff. I stared vacantly at her and her pointy nose—which she took to be a signal that I had a question.

"Yes, Peter, do you have a question? Peter? Peter?"

Truth be told, I didn't know she was talking to me. I couldn't hear a word she said. I thought she was talking and waving at someone else. Only when she made her way over to me did I realize that I was the object of her focus.

"Pappenfuss! Are you watching television while I'm teaching the lesson?"

"Uh . . ." I stalled, trying to remove the earbuds as nonchalantly as possible. "I was just studying." Wrong answer!

"The pastor's son is studying on the Sabbath!"

Here we go.

"And in *my* class!"

"Well, aren't *you* teaching?" I responded. "Am I not supposed to be learning?"

"You," she began in her usual scolding tone, "are *supposed* to be learning *spiritual* things! Not watching movies produced by Hollywood!" Once again, the Junior Sabbath School class was spellbound by another classic interaction between Peter Paul Pappenfuss and Ms. Cracklestaff. Even Jennifer Langley, who chews gum on Sabbath mornings as frequently as she breathes, paused her masticating in anticipation of how I would respond. I couldn't let such restraint go unrewarded.

"I'm watching a nature video about *whales!*" I roared. "Didn't God create *whales?*"

"I don't care what you're watching, SHUT IT OFF and give it to me until the end of class!"

"Fine," I said sweetly, with a sprinkle of sarcasm, as I wrapped the earbuds around the iPod and handed them politely to Ms. Cracklestaff. "I suppose I can just watch you—you're as big as a whale!"

And that's how I arrived at the end of class before anyone else. A raucous chorus of laughter followed me out the door as I made my way to visit my parents' class once again. As per usual, they were not happy to see me. My dad even threatened to send me into Mary's class if I couldn't act my age.

After church we went to the Samfords' for lunch. They live on a farm about twenty miles outside of town. Mom and Dad tried to lecture me about Sabbath School on the way there, and Mary just sat quietly and shook her head at me. But I was too busy watching the whale documentary to pay much attention. Maybe this iPod wasn't such a bad gift after all.

The Samfords have several horses on their farm and even more horse poop. You can smell it when you get close to their home. I'm amazed Melissa doesn't smell like a horse when she comes to school, considering how obsessed she is with them.

"I hope that's not lunch I smell," I said as we pulled into their gravel driveway.

"Peter, so help me, you will *not* act up while we are here," said Dad.

"Just trying to make a joke," I said, putting away the iPod.

"Your sense of humor is crass and rude," said Mary, jabbing a finger into my arm.

"Mary's touching me!" I announced triumphantly.

"Peter, please," said Mom. "You're too old to play that game." Perhaps, but apparently, Mary isn't, because when I grabbed her finger and flung her hand back onto her side of the backseat, she reported my behavior to Mom, which landed me a thirty-minute time-out upon our return home.

Lunch was alright and didn't taste like horse droppings. Mercifully, Melissa was tolerable, and we walked around her farm a bit, looking at horses. I have to admit, they are impressive up close, and they reminded me of the documentary on the Mongols, which was what I would be watching next after the one on whales. The preview for the Mongol documentary showed warhorses racing toward battle, and I imagined myself being able to ride a powerful horse that fast. I wondered if these horses were battle worthy.

"This is *my* horse, Peter," said Melissa, leading me to the last stall in their stable. The horse was all brown with a solitary white patch on its chest. Its eyes gleamed with intelligence, and the musty warm scent of hay wafted from its stall. It was huge, and I couldn't believe Melissa could ride it.

"Wow," I said, patting the horse on its nose. "He looks like a warhorse—do they still make armor for horses? How fast do you ride him?"

Melissa's nostrils flared. "*Her* name is Sally, and we only canter. And as far as armor, we only put ribbons in her hair." Then she stomped off back to the house, leaving me in the stable. When she was out of sight, I leaned in toward Sally and whispered, "If you were my horse, I wouldn't put ribbons in your hair, and we'd ride as fast as you wanted." Sally whinnied her approval.

* * * *

Today is Tuesday, which means it's the second time this week I've had to endure being stared at by students from other classes when I pass them in the hall. Their gazes are a mixture of pity—and fear, as though if somehow they come into contact with me, they might share in the blame when I go down in flames at the contest.

And since I haven't ventured to answer any questions in class yet, my fellow classmates are becoming skeptical of whether my tutoring sessions are having any effect. The skepticism is bolstered by Lucas Snodgrass and his constant commentaries on my progress.

"Awful quiet today, Peter Paul Pappenfuss," said Lucas at lunch. "Maybe you have too many thoughts in your head from tutoring, and they're pushing out your ability to remember how to speak."

There was some nervous laughter, and I really wanted to show Lucas how much my brain remembers how to speak. But as Lucas finished his insult, Principal Purvis walked into the cafeteria and came up to me. He had been doing this since Monday—accosting me in public places.

"Peter, how's the studying going?" he asked. I wasn't sure if he really cared or if he was relishing some sort of personal victory. "Sounds like you haven't been making much progress, if what Lucas says is true. Is it true?" My face burned red hot, and I could feel every eye in the cafeteria on me. I was so mad and frustrated I couldn't speak.

"I told you!" cried Snodgrass, and several people laughed. I wanted to get up, to run out of there, but since Mr. Purvis stood right behind me, I couldn't get up. He smiled and waited for the laughter to die down.

"Maybe we need to add some more time to your tutoring—say another half hour?" I was ready to burst with rage when Ms. Witherspoon came to my rescue. She had been talking to one of the lunch ladies when she noticed our conversation.

"Is there a problem, Principal Purvis?"

He stood up hastily and smiled. "Not at all, Ms. Witherspoon. I was just checking in with Peter here to see how things are progressing."

"He's doing just fine."

The principal nodded and made his way back to his office, which was across from the cafeteria. When he was out of sight, Ms. Witherspoon smiled at me.

"Are you OK, Peter?"

I sighed and nodded.

"Good. OK, class, clean up. Time for recess!"

Recess found me atop the monkey bars with Harley and Gretchen.

Gretchen was telling me about a machine she had heard about that supposedly helps you learn while you sleep.

"I'll do some more research, Peter," she said, pushing her big brown glasses back up on her nose. "I'm not sure how much they cost, but maybe you could rent one."

"Thanks, Gretchen. What I'd really like is to punch Lucas in the face."

"No doubt," agreed Harley. "That's one kid who could use a good punch in the face. Sometimes, it's the only way. But I've got some bad news, Peter—it wouldn't help your cause."

"Why not?"

"Well, I did some asking around with the sixth-graders and found out an interesting fact about 'Snotgrass.'" "Snotgrass" was our new name for Lucas. We thought it captured his personality beautifully.

"What interesting fact is that?" asked Gretchen.

"Did you notice how Mr. Purvis didn't reprimand him at lunch? Well, that's because he's the principal's nephew!"

I wanted to throw something as far as I could. "Spectacular," I muttered.

"Maybe that's why both he and Lucas are on your case. You're already on Principal Purvis's bad side, and now you've stolen their chance to earn the school big money and be heroes at church."

I smiled. "Ha! I should just embrace failure then. You know, squander the chance they want so bad. It could be satisfying."

Gretchen shrugged and adjusted her glasses again. "I dunno, Peter. It might be. But wouldn't it be better to steal that glory for yourself? I mean, you could waste the chance, and they would hate you—and maybe even some other people would. But if you won, that would really shut them up, wouldn't it?"

"Impressive!" agreed Harley.

"I guess so. But, then, there is the matter of me actually being able to win. How likely is that?"

"It depends on how much you put in," said a voice behind us, nearly causing all three of us to fall off the monkey bars out of fright. It was Ms. Witherspoon.

"Teacher," said Harley, composing himself. "How long have you been listening?"

"Long enough to hear something about our principal having a nephew named 'Snotgrass.' " She smiled at us—it wasn't comforting.

"You're not going to tell, are you?" I asked.

"I don't even know who 'Snotgrass' is, so I really don't have anything to tell," she said with a wink, before walking to the school entrance and blowing the whistle signaling that it was time to go in.

"She's alright as far as teachers go, Pete," said Harley, jumping down from the monkey bars and landing ungracefully on his rear. Gretchen and I laughed as we *climbed* down.

"I guess she's OK," I admitted.

"It's got to be hard being a new teacher and having to teach Snotgrass when his uncle is your boss," said Gretchen absentmindedly, as we all walked toward the door.

"I never thought about it that way," I said. And I meant it. That thought bothered me all through the rest of the day and through my tutoring session. After all, Ms. Witherspoon hadn't planned for this to happen; she had to stay at school late too; she had to put up with the principal as much as I did; she had helped program my iPod and rescued me at lunch. A guilty feeling crept over me as I quietly completed my tutoring session on European geography.

When Dad came to pick me up and asked me how the day was, I tried a different response. "Pretty good. Ms. Witherspoon really . . . helped me today." I had never paid a teacher a compliment, especially when they were standing right there. It felt funny. Both my dad and Ms. Witherspoon exchanged silent, shocked glances. "Well, time to go, eh, Dad? Thanks, Ms. Witherspoon."

I walked straight out to the car, leaving them to talk by themselves, and turned on the iPod so Dad wouldn't ask me any more about my day. But I was too lost in thought about the events of the day to notice the sound pumping through my earbuds.

My contemplative attitude didn't last, however. Upon arriving at home, I discovered that my sister had her two abnormal friends, Claudia and Chloe, over to spend the night. I got through supper alright because Dad dominated the conversation, telling everyone about my having a good day. It was embarrassing—especially when Mom even leaned over and squeezed my hand a couple times, beaming with pride. But it was better than listening to the sort of nonsense Claudia and Chloe always talk about.

Believe you me, when my sister and "C-squared" get together, they come up with the weirdest stuff on the planet. One day, they all pretended to be kittens and only "meowed" when Mom asked what they wanted for supper. Instead of calling a psychiatrist, as I suggested, Mom petted each of them on the head and began offering suggestions for supper, eventually deciding on the suggestion that got the most excited "meows."

Another time, all three of them had a tea party right in the middle of the living room. The Mad Hatter from *Alice in Wonderland* would be hard pressed to produce a crazier gathering of nonsense than these three conjured up. For one, they all took on fake English accents, then they all "drank tea" from Mary's toy tea set. I couldn't decide which was more disturbing—the fact that there was no liquid in the cups, because Mom doesn't trust even Dad to eat in the living room, or the fact that all three raved on and on about how good their "tea" was. To top it off, their mad tea party blocked the view of the television.

This evening, however, the name of the game was staring at me through my bedroom doorway. Every time I looked up, they would whisper and giggle. I let it slide twice before hollering down to Mom. "Mom! The Unholy Trinity is bothering me!" That was the first time I had used that name to refer to them. I rather like it. I got it from a sermon Dad gave on a chapter in the book of Revelation. Mom was not impressed.

"Peter Paul Pappenfuss, I don't ever want to hear you call them that again. In the corner with you!" For a change of pace, Mom let me take the dictionary with me during my time-out, so no precious learning time would be wasted.

I wondered about that memory machine Gretchen had talked about at recess. Not that it mattered. I'm not sleeping as well as I usually do. And since tomorrow night is health food night at the Pappenfuss home, I doubt that an empty stomach will make things any better.

CHAPTER TWELVE
BOOM!

Despite having to endure Thursday night's unnatural cuisine—namely, Mom's bean loaf—the rest of my week was surprisingly pleasant.

Dad had to be out late Wednesday and Thursday; he wasn't there to say Good night when I went to bed. I missed him, so I listened to his voice reading Bible verses on the iPod as I went to bed. He had included such texts as " 'Honor your father and your mother' " (Exodus 20:12) and "Hear, my children, the instruction of a father" (Proverbs 4:1). I told Mom these were flagrant attempts by Dad to influence me subliminally. But, for some reason, other texts such as Matthew 5:44, which says we're to love our enemies, and the entire first chapter of Joshua, which talks about being strong and courageous because God is with us, have made more sense to me, even though I've read them before.

I mentioned this at supper on Thursday, and my parents got very quiet and smiled at each other—and then at me. Mary broke the silence, saying that maybe the Holy Spirit was finally starting to work on me and that it was a miracle. I told her it would be an even greater miracle if the Holy Spirit prevented me from smacking her upside the head. Dad laughed, but Mom shook her head.

After supper, my parents had a special prayer with me in my room—and Mary wasn't allowed in. Another miracle. Dad asked me to be honest and wanted me to let them know how I was doing. I couldn't help tearing up—

but I didn't cry. I told them about how frustrated I was. They listened, and Mom even apologized for being too quick with her time-outs, saying that although she doesn't approve of some of my comments, she understands that I am stressed out—and that if I ever need to talk, she's available and that it's OK to be mad, and irritated, and annoyed at people and . . . well, you get the idea.

Dad said I could start picking out some things myself to put on my iPod. He said he had noticed that I hadn't complained about the Mongol documentary and that there were plenty of military documentaries about warriors and battles. He also mentioned he had seen some documentaries on robots, motorcycles, video games, and spaceships. I actually slept well for the first time in two weeks.

Friday, I did my best to ignore Snotgrass's snide remarks and to be nice to Ms. Witherspoon, who—in turn—brought snacks to the tutoring session. Part of the change comes from me listening to memory verses—at least that's what Dad thinks. Maybe he's right. And in the evening, Dad asked me to share my thoughts on some of the scriptures I had been listening to. I did, and he made Mary look up each of them and read them before I made my comments.

At bedtime, both my parents came to tuck me in and pray with me. They sat on either side of my bed with only my Superman nightlight glowing softly in the room. "Thanks for your thoughts at worship tonight, Peter—very insightful," Dad said. "Maybe you should preach at church tomorrow."

I shook my head. "I probably should try getting through Sabbath School before I attempt church."

They both laughed. "Oh, I hope we won't see you in our class tomorrow, Peter," said Mom. "Otherwise, we'll have to buy another adult lesson guide and just start planning on you being there each week."

"Yeah, but what if I get kicked out of *your* class—then where would they send me?" I said.

"To Mary's class," offered Dad with a smile. "Now, it's time for bed. Let's have prayer and ask God to help you keep this good momentum you've been having for the past few days—alright? And, Peter, we want you to know something. Even if you don't win this contest, it's not the end of the world, and we will still be proud of you."

We all closed our eyes, and both Dad and Mom took turns praying for me. Then they hugged and kissed me and shut the door to my room and left me with my thoughts.

Maybe Dad was right—did this contest really matter? The school wasn't in debt; there weren't any building projects underway, and as long as I wasn't the dumbest kid at the contest, it really didn't matter if I won or not. I would compete and, hopefully, win a few rounds before losing. That way, I'd have represented the school well, and then life could get back to normal. The school didn't need me to win—only make a good impression. And with that thought in mind, I felt a burden lifted and fell asleep.

* * * *

"I can't believe you didn't get kicked out of class today," said Melissa Samford as we all left Sabbath School. She was the fifth person to say that after Ms. Cracklestaff's closing prayer, which ended with a praise to God that I hadn't acted up, but was also supplemented with "Please let this not be a sign that he is up to something even more diabolical than usual."

"Thanks, Melissa," I said. Harley and Gretchen caught up with me as I made my way up the steps to the church lobby.

"That was something else, Pete," said Harley. "Your parents didn't drug you, did they?"

"Ha! No, not that I'm aware of anyway."

"So *are* you up to something more diabolical, Peter Paul?" Gretchen wanted to know as we reached the lobby. "I was reading online the other night that some spiders flip over on their backs at night and show different colors to lure in their prey—before flipping back over and biting them and—"

"What on earth are you saying, Gretchen? That Peter is like some sneaky spider waiting to sink his fangs into Ms. Cracklestaff?"

"Well, not literally, you numskull—but in principle," she replied with an air of superiority as she adjusted her glasses. Then she flipped through her enormous study Bible and found Jeremiah 13:23, which says that a leopard can't change its spots. "I'm just saying Peter loves to get into trouble almost as much as we love watching him get into trouble; it's his nature."

I laughed. "Yeah, but Matthew chapter nineteen, verse twenty-six says, ' "with God all things are possible." ' " Harley and Gretchen stared at me dumbfounded. I stopped laughing; a weird feeling stirred in my chest.

"How did you do that?" asked Gretchen. "You don't even have your Bible with you!"

"Wow," exclaimed Harley. "Guess your parents' iPod trick is working, huh?"

"Yeah . . . yeah, I guess it is."

Our moment of awe was disrupted by one of the worst sounds known to mankind coming up the stairs—Lucas Snodgrass's voice.

"Well, well, so Peter Paul Pappenfuss has finally learned a memory verse. At this rate, he will be at the same level as the kindergartners by next week. He's a shoo-in to win the contest next month!"

"Leave us alone, Snotgrass," said Gretchen, closing her Bible. "Don't you have someone else to bother?"

"Sorry! Was I interrupting something? A special moment with your *girlfriend*, Pappenfuss? I knew there was a reason she was so impressed with the one little text you remembered. Her man is finally getting a brain."

Gretchen's cheeks flushed. "I'm *not* his girlfriend!"

"Leave her alone, Lucas," I said with a sigh. "I have to put up with you enough at school; I'd rather not have to look at you at church too."

"Now, now," another voice broke in. "Is there a problem, Peter? You know we are supposed to be loving to one another as Christians, and telling each other that we would rather not see them isn't very loving." Mr. Purvis was wearing a gray suit with white pinstripes and a red tie that didn't match. He put a hand on his nephew's shoulder. But I didn't feel intimidated this time. This was my dad's church—not Mr. Purvis's school.

"You're right, of course," I said, turning to leave. "Isn't it also un-Christian to play favorites since God's love is unconditional? Or don't you and your nephew believe that?" Mr. Purvis turned red, but before he could say anything, Dad showed up.

"Hey, there you are, Peter! I missed you in adult Sabbath School today.

Apparently, this tutoring idea of yours is having an effect, Principal Purvis!"

Mr. Purvis quickly returned to his normal color and forced a smile. "Thank you, Pastor." Then grabbing Lucas's hand, he pulled him out of our group. "Come along Lucas. Let's find your parents so we can get a good seat." Lucas made a face at us as they left.

"You're a smooth one, Pastor Pappenfuss," said Harley.

"What do you mean by that, Mr. O'Brien?"

Harley shook his head. "Nothing—never mind."

"OK, then," said Dad with a puzzled smile, raising an eyebrow at Harley before turning to all of us. "Now, would you two like to sit with our family this morning? You know, to make sure Peter doesn't get into trouble with his sister?" Harley nodded and followed us into the sanctuary, while Gretchen went to ask her parents' permission. They said Yes, and Gretchen made her way down to the second pew, where my family and Harley were, and sat down next to me.

"So, what's your dad talking about today?"

"God," I said, causing Gretchen to roll her eyes. She grabbed the brown hymnal in the shelf on the back of the pew in front of us, and started flipping to the opening hymn listed in the bulletin, just as my dad and the elders walked in.

They came out on the platform, walking in single file—all in black suits. *I wonder if they plan it that way?* I thought. The platform looked nice. There was a fresh flower arrangement in front of the pulpit—compliments of Mrs. Beedaman, according to the bulletin. I looked through the bulletin for any other items of interest, while Dad did the welcome and announcements.

"So, what's happening this week?" asked Gretchen, glancing away from her hymnal.

"Well, let's see," I began, "apparently, the ladies from the Community-Services center are organizing and folding donated clothes Wednesday night at seven o'clock."

"Are you going?" asked Harley.

"No, but your mom is," I replied. We all started laughing, and it wasn't long before Mom whispered something into Mary's ear, and Mary leaned across Harley to share Mom's message.

"Mom says that if you can't be quiet, she will send Harley and Gretchen back to their parents." Then she added her own commentary. "We're in church, Peter; we're supposed to be quiet and reverent."

"Thanks, Saint Mary," said Harley. "Now, why don't you go back to sitting next to Mommy and pray for us." She scowled at him and went back to the Bible-characters coloring book Mom had just bought her.

"You were saying, Peter?" whispered Harley, so Mom wouldn't hear.

"Right, well there isn't much more here, except they spelled the pianist's name—Mrs. Smith—as 'Mrs. Snith.' We all laughed again until Mom gave us a dangerous look. Then the head elder announced it was time to sing the opening hymn.

"Please stand for the opening hymn—number three hundred nine, 'I Surrender All.' "

The hymn was hard to get through without laughing. The Sneldon family was sitting behind us, and both Tommy *and* his dad are easily distracted. While singing, they would trail off, suddenly realize they had lost their place, and mumble along until they realized where we were in the song.

After the hymn, Dad walked to the pulpit and smiled and asked us all to bow our heads. The congregation was still and silent, as they often are after the opening song. I like the atmosphere. It's peaceful, and sometimes I think you can almost feel God's presence in the sanctuary.

"Dear Lord," Dad began, "we thank You for this opportunity to worship You. Please move among us this morning and help us to feel Your presence. We ask You to send Your Holy Spirit to be with us this morning. In Jesus' name, Amen."

Just as Dad ended his prayer, there was a sudden eruption of sound that rattled the windows in the sanctuary—*BOOM!* The pews jumped, along with the people in them. Some women screamed. Sleeping babies cried. Heads turned. Eyes widened. Ears rang. And one little voice in the balcony cried out, "He's here! The pastor prayed for God to come, and HE'S HERE!"

A few people chuckled nervously as though they weren't sure if the little voice was right or not. The rest of us were too stunned to make a move or a sound. Then our stupor was broken by one of the eighth-graders, Chris

Watts, who burst through the main sanctuary doors shouting, "The school's blown up! THE SCHOOL'S BLOWN UP!"

Immediately, a chorus of cheering children resounded through the church—there was no time to quiet them. People all over the place got up and raced (as reverently as possible) out to the church parking lot to see what had happened. My dad led the way, along with several elders.

"Well, come on, kids—no use staying in here," said Mom, getting us all up and leading us outside with the rest of the congregation.

Our school is located across the parking lot from the church, and as we exited the main church entrance, we were greeted by the usual sight of the gymnasium and the adjoining structure, which includes the cafeteria and classrooms—with one exception.

There was a smoking crater in the side of the gym!

It was surrounded by gawking church members who absentmindedly tried to hold their exuberant kids from getting too close, while others counted heads to make sure no one was missing.

"Wow!" said Harley, awestruck. It captured the mood well.

"What happened?" I asked as we approached the main body of believers gathered around the hole in the school. People shook their heads in confusion. I could see Dad and a couple of elders close to the hole; the head deacon, Donald Reichquist, was coming out of the hole in the wall. He had a handkerchief over his nose and mouth and was coughing. After composing himself, he said something to Dad, and then they stepped away from the billowing black smoke before addressing us.

"We have already called the fire department," began Dad, "and they should be here in a few minutes. As for what happened, it appears that the boiler has blown up." A few people gasped.

"Awesome!" I said, without thinking—earning several dirty looks from the more pious among us. Also, my comment was not lost on my mother. She seized my arm and looked at me square in the eye.

"Peter, so help me, if you had anything to do with this—"

"That's right, Mom," I interrupted coolly, "not only can I get one hundred percent on tests by randomly guessing, but I also specialize in explosives and espionage. While you were singing the opening hymn, I quietly slipped away by crawling under the pews and planted dynamite all over the school and . . ."

"OK. OK," she said, releasing me and taking a deep breath. "I'm sorry. But for goodness' sake, Peter, this is not what I would call 'awesome.' It's . . . it's . . ." she trailed off as she stared at the black hole.

"Terrible," said a woman in a blue dress standing next to us.

"Frightful," muttered an elderly gentleman toward the front of the crowd.

"A travesty!" cried a familiar voice that belonged to a man with a bulging vein in his forehead, who was making his way to the scene and clutching his chest.

"Awesome," whispered Harley. Gretchen and I smiled.

Principal Purvis looked as white as a sheet against the color of his dark gray suit; he wobbled as he walked.

"Is he going to faint, Mommy?" asked Mary.

"Awesome," said Gretchen. Mom gave her a look, but spared her a lecture.

"Pastor Pappenfuss!" cried Mr. Purvis, making his way to my dad. "Our school is ruined!" Dad did his best to calm him down—along with others in the crowd who were beginning to murmur.

"Now, now, it doesn't appear that anyone was hurt, and we can be thankful for that," Dad said, placing a reassuring hand on Mr. Purvis. "But we need to pray that our school will be alright. And in light of this disaster, why don't we have a quick word of prayer right now and dismiss church for today." Dad prayed, and this time the only noise that followed his "Amen" was the sound of fire sirens.

"So, is church over, then?" asked Gretchen. Mom nodded.

"Yes, dear, it is. Why don't you and Harley go find your parents. I think I see them toward the front there. Just let them know you're safe." As they ran off, Mom grabbed Mary's hand.

"Alright, then," she said, "let's go see what your father's plans are." We waded through the people who were beginning to leave; several people stopped Mom, asking her what she thought they should do.

"I'm sure I don't know," she answered. "No doubt, we'll know more after the firemen have assessed the damage and we have had a chance to discuss options for repair."

When we finally reached Dad, the firemen were holding Mr. Purvis back from going into the smoking hole. "Now, sir, we've told you that it may still be dangerous. Please go and wait with your pastor and the rest of the congregation."

"But I'm the principal," he shouted, fighting against their grip. "I have a right to see inside my own school!"

"Please, Mr. Purvis," said my dad, noticeably stressed. It wasn't enough his church service had been interrupted by a freak explosion, but now the principal of the church school was causing more trouble. "You can see it as soon as they say it's safe."

But Mr. Purvis was having none of it. All at once, he seemed to see me for the first time. He suddenly stopped fighting against the fireman and whirled around to face me. Dad firmed up his grip on my shoulder. "Pastor, this boy of yours had better not have had anything to do with this disaster. We *all* know what happened at the camporee—creating fireballs seems to be a gift of his."

Dad cut me off before I could protest.

"In spite of Peter's many gifts, such as being able to guess one hundred percent on tests, I'm sure he hasn't taken up explosives—at least not at home. And the camporee incident was not his fault, and you know that. However, your fiery anger is less than accidental," Dad told him. He let the silence sink in for a moment, then continued, "What has happened is horrible, stressful, and shocking. We are all upset, but explosive outbursts are not going to solve the problem—nor is running into danger. I'm sure you would agree that we need to model the right behavior for all the school children—*and* their parents who will no doubt be discussing today's events over Sabbath lunch."

Mr. Purvis's right eye twitched, and he exhaled. Then, without a word, he made his way to his car and drove home. After the firemen made sure the area was safe and blocked off access to what was formerly the boiler room, we drove home as well.

CHAPTER THIRTEEN
THE COST

Dad spent the rest of the weekend on the phone, preparing for an emergency board meeting Sunday afternoon. The meeting was to start at three o'clock, and Dad's bosses were going to be there.

"Is Dad going to get fired?" I asked Mom Sunday morning after breakfast, while she washed the dishes.

"No, honey," she replied, drying off a casserole dish. "The people who are coming are there to help pastors and churches. And by the looks of it, we will need all the help we can get."

"Is Mr. Purvis going to be there?"

"Yes, Peter."

Dad's meeting lasted for five hours. Mom called his cell phone every hour to check in, and the answer was always the same. I could hear it since she had the phone in the kitchen on speaker the third time she called.

"Not yet, sweetheart—I've got to go." I could hear heated voices in the background and even the crashing of a steel folding chair.

"Sounds like a wrestling match," I said—wishing I could be there.

"That's probably not too far from the truth, Peter," Mom replied, hanging up the phone.

"I wonder if Mr. Purvis is wearing a mask or tights like they do on television."

Mom raised an eyebrow. "Peter, are you watching wrestling? You know that's not allowed in this house."

"I know," I said. "That's why I watch it at Harley's."

After Mom made a call to Harley's mother, she suggested that we all play a game. Mary wanted to play Candyland, and for once we were in agreement. I realize Candyland is a game for little kids, but my folks added new rules a couple of years ago. We play with real candy. Therefore, it is always the first game to be suggested when we're asked to choose. Mom and Dad allow it only on special occasions, and since this weekend was so full of stress, Mom agreed to our request in hopes of lightening our hearts. We needed it. I wasn't sure if Dad could hold his own at the meeting as well as he had that morning in the parking lot.

At eight o'clock, Dad called to say we should get ready to come pick him up. Mom had dropped him off earlier that afternoon, since she had had errands to run. She had thought the meeting wouldn't last more than two hours. So when Dad called, we packed up the game and drove over to the church. When no one came out after twenty minutes, I was elected to go inside as a scout to see the status of the meeting.

I felt like a spy—which is why I agreed to do it. I slowly opened the door to the church and crept in. It was mostly dark inside the foyer, except for the lights in the hallway that led to the boardroom. I could hear voices, but they were more subdued and tired than the ones I had heard before on the phone. I crept softly down the hall, passed the pastoral offices, the Cradle Roll and Primary rooms, and the library. The boardroom was the last room on the right, and the door was slightly open.

I got down on my hands and knees right by the doorframe and peeked through the crack to see what was going on. There were a lot of black suits and even darker expressions. Mr. Purvis was silent. Dad was at the end of the table, scribbling some notes, and everyone else seemed to be waiting for him to finish.

"OK," said Dad, making one last mark on his notepad with his pen, "here is where we stand. The cost to replace the boiler, as estimated by the contractor, is forty-five thousand dollars." I almost gasped at the figure, but put my hand over my mouth and kept listening as Dad continued his summary.

"With the funds pledged yesterday and this morning, the church can raise ten thousand dollars, but even that is going to be tricky, because we are still paying off the new parking lot, and donors are stretched thin. The conference can grant us twenty-five thousand dollars, making a total of thirty-five thousand dollars. This leaves us ten thousand dollars short—with another major problem." Dad nodded toward an older gentleman with a buzz haircut and thick frames. "Our education director, Mr. Tibbs, has pointed out that winter is on its way, and since the boiler provides heat to our school, we could be forced to shut down the facility for the year." This time I did gasp, and I heard my dad pause abruptly.

I tore back down the hallway as quietly as possible and dashed back to the car breathless. "Peter?" Mom asked. "Are you alright? Where's your father? Is the meeting over?"

"Um . . . I don't know," I said between gasps for air. "Maybe."

"Why are you so out of breath, Peter?" asked Mary from the backseat. "Are you out of shape? You know that your body is the temple of the Holy Spirit and you should treat it better. Maybe you should finish your homework earlier, so you can get some exercise."

I regained my breath and turned around to face Mary. "Good idea. Maybe I could start by coming back there and—"

"Peter!" snapped Mom. "I don't want to hear it. Now, hop in the backseat. Here comes your father, and if I hear so much as a peep out of you, you will get exercise by running around the house for an hour!"

I grumbled and crawled back next to Mary, who was beaming. "Mary," I said, looking at her sweet face and pigtails, "you can try fake crying, but just know that my fist will be real when it hits your arm." Her smile faded, and she looked out the window. Dad opened the door and looked at me curiously but said nothing.

"How was the meeting?" asked Mom. "I sent Peter in to check on things, but he came back all out of breath and didn't say much." Dad got in and gave me a look but said nothing before turning back to Mom.

"I don't want to talk about it. I'll tell you when we get home." Mom nodded and began to drive. No one said a word on the way home. Especially me. I knew everyone wished they knew what went on in that meeting, but if they knew what I did, they'd wish differently.

I may not be a genius at math, but I knew enough to add up the numbers and figure out the consequences discussed at Dad's meeting. The school needed ten thousand dollars or it would have to close. By some strange co-incidence, the winner of the academic contest would win ten thousand dollars. The implications for my future were frightening, and I hoped no one else on the church board was thinking what I was thinking.

CHAPTER FOURTEEN
CONFESSION

The tension at my house was enough to drive a person mad. People were snapping at the slightest things, and acts of violence toward little sisters were on the rise. A few dishes had been dropped and broken out of sheer nerves. Conversations consisted of "Pass the salt," "Do your homework," and prayers before bedtime. And it had been only four days since the boiler blew up.

School wasn't much better. Monday, there was no school except for my tutoring session. We were doing science that week. I was excited about science—what with all the acids, chemicals, body parts, and Bunsen burners. But since the boiler exploded, Mr. Purvis has forbidden any sort of science experiments and has restricted us to textbook-only science classes. If I fail this contest because of a science question, I'm blaming him.

Kids were happy about missing school, but they did not enjoy coming back. Mr. Purvis was on edge, telling everyone—even the mailman—to "BE QUIET!" Teachers taught their lessons like they were zombies. Ms. Witherspoon relied heavily on worksheets for our education this week, and even recess had the life sucked out of it thanks to relay races, running laps, and calisthenics.

Then there was the rumor mill to contend with.

"My dad says that the school is *doomed*!" announced one seventh-grader in a cheerful voice at lunch.

"It's a sign from the Lord, because we aren't strict with our dress code," said a fourth-grader in the hallway during a fire drill. "At least that's what my grandma says."

"I heard it'll cost a million dollars to fix," said a first-grader in the lobby, as he waited for his mom to pick him up after school.

"No," disagreed his friend, "it'll cost a KA-JILLION dollars!" They both laughed and agreed.

"It might as well be a 'ka-jillion' dollars," I muttered, as I went for my tutoring session. So far, I had spent Monday through Wednesday just reading quietly for two hours. I didn't expect today to be any different.

Ms. Witherspoon was doodling absentmindedly on her desk calendar when I came in. She looked up and smiled weakly. "Hi, Peter. How are you?"

"I've been better. How are *you*?"

She exhaled deeply. "About the same as you, I suppose. Come here and sit down. I'd like to talk to you." I complied, and she began, carefully choosing her words. "Peter Paul, you know that there are rumors flying around because of the boiler situation, right?"

"Yeah," I said annoyed. "I just heard it's going to cost a 'ka-jillion' dollars to fix it."

She smiled but looked serious. "No, it's not. But it *is* going to cost ten thousand dollars." I felt my stomach churn. I think ten thousand is now my least favorite number. Ms. Witherspoon continued. "Peter, I just want you to be aware that some people may look to you as an answer for the school's financial needs. However," she went on before I could interrupt, "I want you to know that the only thing that matters is that you do your best."

"Thanks for the cliché," I said.

She sighed and put her hand on my shoulder. "Peter, I know it doesn't take the stress away, but it's important to know that I am not going to put that kind of pressure on you—OK?" I nodded. "Good! Then let's get to work."

After three hours of studying cells, electricity, and acids, I think it's safe to say that I have lost all desire to work in a science-related field. What I wouldn't give for a comic book! Dad showed up on time, and I was told to wait in the car while he and Ms. Witherspoon had a "little chat."

In case you haven't noticed it in your own experience, whenever someone wants to have a "little chat," it usually means that they want to talk about *big* trouble in a short amount of time. More specifically, trouble that involves *you*. Dad took fifteen minutes, and then we began the trip home. He didn't say a word to me and looked lost in thought. When he failed to stop at a stop sign and cut off a pair of senior citizens in their minivan, I knew he had things on his mind.

Horns blared. Dad gunned it to avoid a collision, and the senior citizens screamed—or at least that's what they looked like they were doing when we passed in front of them at Mach 5. Dad's knuckles were white, and he exhaled heavily. I stared at him with my eyebrows raised.

"Do you want me to drive?" I asked.

"No, Peter," said Dad sharply without looking at me, "and I'm in no mood for silliness."

"Well, I'm in no mood to end my life. And judging by the looks of them, neither were those old people."

"Peter . . . ," Dad said in one of his more foreboding tones.

"Fine," I said and looked out the window at the passing houses until we reached ours.

Supper was a joy—a killjoy. No one spoke. Not even Mary, who delights in telling stories of her superiority to make me feel inferior. At the beginning, Mom tried by asking how Dad's day had been. I answered for him, telling Mom about our near-death experience.

"Boy, Mom, you should have seen him!" I said. "I think we were going a hundred miles an hour through that four-way stop!" Mom wasn't impressed, and neither was Dad, who told Mom he would talk to her later about what his day had been like. After that, the mood in the house changed to that of a funeral parlor.

I finished my food quickly—without seconds—and dismissed myself to my room. I was so tired, I figured I'd go to bed early and hopefully wake up to a happier household. That was, if I could manage some rest and avoid dreaming about the number ten thousand and what it means for my life.

After an hour of restlessly lying there and playing absentmindedly with my Transformers, there was a knock on the door.

"Go away, Mary! Why don't you find the mother ship and head back to Planet Stupid?"

"It's Dad—and for the last time, your sister is not an alien, and she is not stupid. Now, can I come in?" His tone was gentle, so I granted his request.

The door opened, and he came in. He was holding a tray with two steaming mugs of hot chocolate and fresh chocolate-chip cookies.

"Mind if I hang out here for a little while?" he asked.

"It depends," I said with a smile. "Are those cookies for me?"

"Some of them, but I thought I'd have a few, too, if it's alright."

"Fair enough," I said, setting my Transformers aside. Dad set the tray down on my desk and then handed me a mug before grabbing his own and some of the cookies. We ate and drank in silence for a while before he spoke.

"I'm sorry for flying off the handle today, Peter—"

"And nearly getting us killed?"

He laughed. "Yes, and for nearly getting us killed. How frightened *were* those elderly people you saw?"

"Terrified," I answered. He shook his head.

"Oh dear, those poor people!"

I shrugged as I reached for my fifth cookie. "Well, maybe they needed the excitement," I said, trying to be positive.

"No one needs that much excitement," Dad replied, also reaching for another cookie.

"Sounds like you have quite a bit of excitement with that crater in the side of the school," I offered.

Dad set his mug down on my nightstand and nodded. "I wanted to talk to you about that, Peter. I spoke with Ms. Witherspoon, and she told me what she told you—about the ten thousand dollars and the need the school has. Peter, I want to reaffirm what she said and let you know that your mother and I feel the same—but I do want to make a request of you."

"What sort of request?" I asked, setting down my cookies and reclining on my pillow while I held the warm cup of cocoa with both hands.

"Well, as you may have heard," Dad said, giving me a knowing look that made me uncomfortable, "the school needs ten thousand dollars to fix the boiler situation."

"So raise the money; we have some rich people in the church, don't we?"

"Peter," said Dad in one of his you-know-better-than-that tones, "we have already raised money from the church and the conference, and we're still ten thousand dollars short."

"Oh, " I said.

"Now, I know that the winner of this contest of yours gets ten thousand dollars—"

"You want me to win, don't you?" I said, sitting up, ready to get angry.

"Peter, everyone wants you to win, but that's not exactly what I'm asking."

I calmed down and sat back against my pillow. I took a sip of hot chocolate. "So what *are* you asking?" I said.

"Peter, this problem affects the whole church. If we can't fix the boiler before the weather turns cold, then the school runs the risk of closing."

My mouth went dry, and I think my heart stopped beating. "You're going to close the school?" I shouted, sitting straight up, nearly dumping hot chocolate all over the bed.

Dad waved at me to calm down and to keep it down. "*Ssshh*, Peter! Your sister can't hear this. And, no, we are not closing down the school—not by God's grace. It's just a looming danger that we have to work with."

"Rats," I said, wondering what life would be like with no school, no learning, and no Principal Purvis.

"Please listen to me."

I sighed and motioned for him to continue.

"As I was saying, this is a problem that affects the whole church, and it's not fair for you to bear the burden of everybody. So that's why I need your permission to tell the church this Sabbath about what we're facing and about the opportunity you have."

This time I did spill my hot chocolate—all over my pants and on my bedspread. I leaped up as the heat soaked through my pants onto my legs. "OW! OW! OW! OW!" I yelled, prancing around the room, trying to get my pants off and end the burning that was running down my legs. In five minutes, I had managed to peel them off and get into a change of clothes, while Dad took care of the bedspread. Mom didn't say a word to us as we put my pants and the bedspread in the hamper. She just shook her head.

To my great fortune, the only clean bedspread was an old one of my Mom's that was pea green with blue flowers on it.

"Sorry, Peter," said Dad, as he made the bed. "I will make sure you have your usual bedspread tomorrow."

"I may not want it then, Dad—a night with this thing, and I might wake up wanting to play with Mary's Barbies." We sat down again—this time without hot chocolate—and continued our conversation.

"Why on *earth* would you tell the church?" I asked in disbelief. "My life is hard enough as it is without the 'brethren' knowing."

"I want to tell the church because they can pray for you, encourage you, and support you as a church family should."

"You don't think they'd lynch me in the parking lot, instead? Or send letter bombs?"

Dad shook his head. "No, Peter, I think that the majority of the people would rally around you and support you."

"The majority, but what about the minority?" I asked. "I know at least two people who have made it their hobby to make me miserable."

"There are always a few people who want to make our lives miserable, Peter, but those people have issues, too, and you can't take it personally. Sometimes when people are dealing with their own hurts in life, they look for a target to take out their frustration on. I'm sorry you have become a target, but I think you'll find that most people will be supportive."

"What's in this for me?" I asked. "And don't tell me 'the satisfaction of a job well done.' "

Dad laughed. "Well, besides more support—what else do you want?"

"Well, how about this," I began. "My life has been dominated by study these past few weeks. If I agree to this—even if I don't win—you tell Ms. Witherspoon to make my homework load a little lighter for the rest of the semester."

Dad thought for a moment before speaking. "OK. I'll see what I can do." Then he called Mom upstairs, and they had prayer with me before tucking me into bed. They gave me hugs and kisses, and they both let me know that even if I didn't win, they would find other ways to support the school. I felt teary-eyed as they said Good night, but not as bad as the last time we had a heart-to-heart. I sincerely hoped Dad's idea would go as he thought it would.

CHAPTER FIFTEEN
THE ANNOUNCEMENT

Dad made the announcement at the end of his sermon, just before the benediction. He called me to the front and told the congregation essentially what he had told me on Monday night. The effect was a mixture of shock, hope, and horror. After the announcement, Dad invited people to come to the front and pray for me.

"Let's gather around Peter here and lay hands on him as a church family and lift him up before God as he prepares to represent our church at the contest in a couple weeks."

At first, no one moved. Then, slowly, Mom and Mary, the O'Briens, and a few of the elders began to make their way to the front. Their example inspired others, and before long, I was surrounded by dark suits and dresses and hundreds of hands reaching toward me. I hoped they would be gentle.

We all knelt down, and Dad put his hand on my head, because every other part of me was already taken—and began to pray.

"Dear Lord, You know the situation our school faces, and You know the situation Peter faces. We ask You to watch over him in a special way. Give him wisdom, strength, and courage and help us to support him no matter what happens. We dedicate him to You now, in Jesus' name. Amen."

After people took their seats, Dad signaled for the closing hymn, and we walked out together while people sang.

"Are we leaving early so people don't try to mob us in the parking lot?" I asked.

"No, Son, you are going to stand at the door with me and greet people."

"Oh! Could I go home, instead?"

"No."

As usual, the deacons dismissed the front row first before making their way to the back pews. Slowly, one by one, people made their way to the door. I wasn't sure what to expect.

The first people out the door were a middle-aged couple who shook my hand and gave me a polite smile. Then they whispered something to my dad who simply responded, "I'm sure he will."

The next few people had similar greetings for me and my father, and it wasn't doing much to bolster my spirits. Then came Mr. Crabtree, the school secretary's father. His hair didn't grow on his head anymore, but rather out his ears. His gaze was menacing, and his face bore the kind of expression people make when someone steps on their feet. He also walks with a cane that he has no doubt used to beat children.

"Pappenfuss!" he snapped at me. Dad took a step closer and put his arm around me. "How are you this morning, Jasper?" asked Dad politely.

Mr. Crabtree scoffed. "I was fine until I found out that the future of Christian education in Davenport depends on this juvenile."

"My name is Peter," I said firmly, trying to be polite.

Mr. Crabtree raised his eyebrows. "Well, your name will be 'mud' if you fail—and don't talk back to your elders. I don't appreciate sass." He brandished his cane for a moment.

"Thanks for your concern," said Dad, moving him along.

Mr. Crabtree muttered to himself and hobbled his way out of the lobby to wherever it is they allow him to live.

"What a ray of sunshine!" I said. "I can see where Ms. Crabtree gets her charm." Harley, Gretchen, and several classmates were next. They all wished me well, although much of their enthusiasm left something to be desired. After them, came more polite people and a few genuinely supportive church leaders, which I appreciated.

Bringing up the rear, unfortunately, was Principal Purvis and Lucas. Lucas's parents were also coming. They didn't even look at me as they walked out. Instead, they talked loudly enough for us to hear.

"So, Lucas," said Mr. Purvis, "would you like me to homeschool you and your friends next year?"

"Oh, that would be wonderful," he replied snidely. "I'm sure it would be a better education than I'm getting now." They continued on like that as they sauntered out the door. Dad rubbed his temples and sighed.

"Don't worry, Dad," I said, putting a hand on his shoulder. "Lucas doesn't have any friends, so Mr. Purvis couldn't make a living teaching just him." Dad gave me a half smile.

"It's alright, Peter. Looks like you have one last person," and he nodded toward the last person in line.

It was a little, elderly lady wearing a floral print dress and a red hat. She wasn't a church member, but sometimes helped the Community Services ladies, and she always wore a smile. Today was no different. She beamed from ear to ear, her wrinkles giving way to a kind spirit that put me at ease.

She clasped my hand tightly. I could feel something in her grip. She looked straight into my eyes and spoke softly. "God will bless you. Don't worry. I know He loves you very much. If you get discouraged, just look at this little note and trust in Him." She released her grip, bowed her head politely, then shook my dad's hand before making her way to her car. I watched her leave, then looked down at the note she had given me.

In my hand was a torn piece of the bulletin on which she had written, "Daniel 3:17, 18." Dad peeked over my shoulder.

"Hmmm . . . very interesting. Do you know that text, Pete?" I shook my head. "Look it up if you get a chance; I'd like to know what it says."

"OK," I said, putting it into my pocket.

* * * *

When we got home, I placed the Daniel text on my dresser, figuring I'd read it later. But I forgot all about it when the "phonathon" started. The entire weekend was full of phone calls. People called to pledge their support, give advice, make demands, and offer opinions, arguments, and orders. Mercifully, I didn't have to field any of the calls. But Dad did.

On Sunday, around noon, Dad unplugged the phone in the kitchen, living room, and office—and then settled into his favorite chair—a green monstrosity from the eighties he bought in college. I sat down on the couch next to him and suggested that we leave town like the Von Trapp family in *The Sound of Music* when the Nazis were taking control of Austria. Dad said he was impressed with my historical analogy, but it wasn't practical and that comparing the church congregation to the Nazis wasn't a good idea.

"Good idea or not," I replied, "they have invaded our weekend."

"That's true, Peter," said Dad, standing up, stretching, and making his way to the entryway closet. "Well, maybe we *can* run away for a little while. Do you think your mom and sister would like to take a trip to Dairy Queen?"

"Perhaps Mom would, but as for Mary, you can never tell. She isn't like the rest of us, and I've found that sugar makes her even more intolerable than usual."

"What's that?" asked Mary, who had appeared at the top of the stairs. "Aren't *you* the one who ate so much cake at Harley's birthday party last summer that it made you sick?"

"Not really."

"I heard you threw up nine times."

"Ugly rumors."

"I heard they still have it on video."

"Alright, you two! Get your coats, and I'll get your mother," ordered Dad. "And *please* try to talk about something pleasant while I'm gone." As soon as Dad disappeared up the stairs, Mary started up again.

"Honestly, Peter, you really need to work on your behavior. You are so rude." As she continued, I quietly grabbed her white coat out of the closet and held it as a gentleman would—offering to help her put it on. This stopped her short, and she nodded her approval. Flinging her golden hair over her shoulder with an air of superiority, she said, "Thank you, Peter. Isn't it much better to *behave* for once?"

"Quite," I agreed, placing the coat over her shoulders. But before she could put her arms in her sleeves, I wrapped the sleeves around her and tied them in the best knot I could think of.

"Peter, you jerk!" she cried, twisting and turning and eventually falling to the floor like a crazy person trying to escape a straightjacket.

"Now, now, Mary," I said in my most self-important tone, "calm down. If you are this hyper now, just imagine what will happen when you have ice cream."

CHAPTER SIXTEEN
MR. POPULAR

"Peter, I believe it's your turn to pick our devotional text this morning," said Mom, handing me the Bible.

Every morning, we have a quick family devotion with Mom and take turns selecting a text to read and apply to our lives. Mom, Mary, and I were sitting in our usual places on the couch, all dressed and ready for school, when Mom reminded me it was my turn.

"Oh . . . , I forgot. Mary can have my turn."

Mom shook her head. "Peter, I am not going to let you pawn off your responsibilities on your sister. Now, come on. You've been studying; I'm sure you have a text in mind." She set the Bible on my lap. It was a black, leather-bound NIV Bible with gold-trimmed pages. It had all kinds of study helps in it and weighed five tons. I looked at Mom, annoyed. She just tapped the Bible and motioned for me to get on with it.

Normally, I would have a text picked out, but I have been dreading this morning. After all the calls over the weekend and Dad's grand announcement at church, I'm not sure what to expect at school—picking a Bible text for morning worship has been the last thing on my mind.

"Fine," I said, sitting up. Without breaking my annoyed gaze at Mom, I opened the Bible and plopped my finger down on one of the pages. "This one."

"Peter Paul, you don't even know what you picked! You know that isn't the right way to study the Bible," said Mary, crossing her arms.

"Why not?" I snapped. "Doesn't it say somewhere that *all* Scripture is inspired?"

Mary stuck out her tongue, and Mom sighed and motioned for me to hand her the Bible. "Very well," she said, looking to see what random text my finger landed on. "Hmm," she muttered to herself with a smile.

"What does it say, Mom?" asked Mary, peeking over Mom's shoulder. "Did Peter pick something inappropriate?"

"*You're* inappropriate," I retorted. "Besides, how can there be something 'inappropriate' in the Bible?"

"Children, calm down. This is family worship—not family feud. Now, about this text you picked, Peter. Normally, I would agree with Mary that random finger-pointing is a little haphazard for Bible study. But in this case, maybe God was directing your finger. Yes, I really think that this text will—"

"Ow! Stop it, Peter!" yelled Mary.

"Peter, what on earth are you doing?" asked Mom.

"He's poking my arm!" cried Mary.

"I'm doing nothing of the sort," I replied. "God's directing my finger."

"Young man, if you don't leave your sister alone, God is going to start directing *my hand*, and you *don't* want that to happen."

"Good point," I said, folding my hands while Mary rubbed her arm and glared at me. "So, how about that text?"

Mom gave me a look before continuing. "The text, Peter Paul, is Joshua chapter one, verse six. I'll read through verse nine. ' "Be strong and courageous, because you will lead these people to inherit the land I swore to their forefathers to give them. Be strong and very courageous. Be careful to obey all the law my servant Moses gave you; do not turn from it to the right or to the left, that you may be successful wherever you go. Do not let this Book of the Law depart from your mouth; meditate on it day and night, so that you may be careful to do everything written in it. Then you will be prosperous and successful. Have I not commanded you? Be strong and courageous. Do not be terrified; do not be discouraged, for the LORD your God will be with you wherever you go." ' "

Mom paused a few moments, letting us contemplate what she had read.

Then she said, "Well, where do you see God wanting you to be strong and courageous today?"

Mary was quick to reply. "First, I have a brother who bothers me whom I have to put up with." She stared at me just to make sure none of us confused the brother she was talking about with some other brother we weren't aware of. "Then," she continued, "there is the issue with the school—God is asking us to be courageous in the face of *overwhelming* odds." She looked at me again, just in case anyone was unsure why the odds were so unfavorable.

"You're cruisin' for a bruisin', pigtails," I said coolly. Mary stroked her pigtails and looked pleadingly at Mom.

"Peter?"

"Yes?"

"What about you? What do you hear God saying to you in this verse? Can you think of a situation that He wants you to have peace in?"

"Nope."

"Peter!"

I knew what she wanted me to say—all mothers know what they want their kids to say when they ask them questions. I don't see the point of mothers asking questions at all, really. Like last year, when Harley and I played baseball in the backyard and I threw the ball through the living room window, Mom asked me, "Did one of you boys throw the ball through the window?" Honestly, what did she think happened? That the ball climbed the tree in our yard, ran along one of the branches, and threw itself through the window to end its misery? Maybe. Harley *does* throw like a girl.

"Peter, I'm waiting," said Mom, snapping me out of my trance.

"Yeah," I sighed, "I know a situation. I just don't want to talk about it."

Mom paused, then nodded as she closed the Bible.

"Fair enough—as long as you know, and as long as you remember God is with you no matter where you go." We each said a short prayer for our family, for the school, and for our day—then went out to the curb to wait for the bus. The bus was late as usual. Mary tried to use this time to scold me for my behavior, but I threw on the old iPod and tuned her out.

When the bus came, it was mostly full. I took my seat in the back next to

Harley, Gretchen, and Big Calvin. The rest of my class was sitting in the middle.

"What are you listening to today, Pete?" asked Calvin.

I paused my iPod and sighed. "English grammar." There was a collective groan of sympathy. "Thanks guys—it's pretty bad. I mean our language is so confusing. Like, trying to figure out when to use the word *that* and when to use the word *which*. The rule is that you use *that* when introducing essential clauses and *which* with nonessential clauses—but if they're nonessential, then why use them? But, obviously, they *are* essential because they were used in the first place!" I slammed the iPod down on my lap in frustration. By this time, I was receiving several blank stares.

"So . . . uh . . . ," stuttered Calvin, "what's a clause?"

"Really, Peter, the only clause we know is Santa Claus," added Sam.

"The simple version?"

"Please," said Calvin.

"A clause is a part of a sentence that can stand by itself."

"So, what's an essential clause?" asked Gretchen.

"A clause with no commas around it."

"So, . . . a nonessential clause has commas?" asked Harley.

"Exactly."

"Oh, man, I think you need to put that iPod down. The fact that we are having this conversation gives me the creeps." Several people nodded, and I heard some whispering going on.

I shrugged. "I wish I could, friends, but the contest is closing in, and besides, I'd rather listen to this garbage than the latest remarks from Snotgrass—who I believe is our next pick up." Another groan permeated the bus as the driver stopped in front of Lucas's house. I put my earbuds back in.

* * * *

"Alright, students," said Ms. Witherspoon after our morning prayer, "you have five minutes to review last week's spelling assignment, then we are going to have a spelling bee." The joy in the classroom was overpowering.

"Aw, man, I thought I was done with those words," whined Wesley from the front row.

"Don't tell me you forgot them already," said Ms. Witherspoon, crossing her arms with a smirk.

"It was an eventful weekend—especially church," he replied. The class fell silent except for the evil glee buzzing around Snotgrass's desk.

"Indeed, it was," said Lucas, reclining in his chair. "I found the prayer time a bit much—especially since the sermon went so long." I was ready to throw my chair at him before Ms. Witherspoon intervened.

"OK, Lucas, that's enough. And don't lean so far back in your chair; it isn't *smart*." I thought I saw Ms. Witherspoon wink at me, and I definitely saw the glee leave Lucas's face as he returned to a normal sitting position. "Now then, five minutes, class. Hurry and review, and then we'll get to work."

The five minutes went swiftly, and before I knew it, I heard Ms. Witherspoon calling me to the front to start things off. I slowly made my way up, realizing that this was what it would feel like—only worse—at the academic contest, with my intelligence, or lack thereof, on display for all. Ms. Witherspoon mercifully chose Harley to go against me. Harley is good at math and science, but he spells his own name differently every time he submits an assignment. I had better not mess this up.

The rest of the class was unusually attentive for a spelling bee—no doubt aware, as I was, that this exercise would be a foretaste of the academic contest that would determine their academic future.

"OK, boys," began Ms. Witherspoon, holding the spelling book in hand at her desk while Harley and I stood in front of the white board, "the first word is *reading*. 'I enjoying reading the newspaper.' *Reading*. Harley, you will go first."

Harley spent a few moments sounding out the word before offering his fateful attempt. " '*Reading*.' R-E-E-D-I-N-G." The sniggering in the class told him immediately he was wrong. He took a bow—much to everyone's delight—and sat down. Even Ms. Witherspoon had to fight back a grin.

"I'm sorry, but that is not correct—as you have guessed." Then she turned to me and was more serious. "Peter, your turn. *Reading*."

I took a breath, then faced my classmates. " '*Reading*.' R-E-A-D-I-N-G."

The silence that greeted me made me feel panicky, but the scowl on Lucas's face told me I was right.

"Very good, Peter! That is correct. Now, who should go next?"

I managed to defeat Calvin, Jennifer, and Wesley before the inevitable happened. Ms. Witherspoon asked if there were any volunteers to go against me, and a single hand shot up. Snotgrass.

"I'd be delighted to beat Pappenfuss," he said with poison in his voice. He made his way to the front. There was an awkward moment, and Ms. Witherspoon clearly looked as though she wasn't sure about this. She cleared her throat and began to read the first word, when a sharp knock came at the door.

Ms. Witherspoon opened the door to reveal our church's head deacon, Mr. Reichquist. He wore a big grin and stepped inside.

"Hello, class, how is everyone today?" We gave him the usual semicomatose "Good morning" greeting that classrooms always do.

"Mr. Reichquist, it's nice to see you. Can I ask what brings you to class?"

He walked right up to me. "This young man right here."

Lucas sneered. "Did you discover that he blew up the school, after all?"

"Oh no, no," said Mr. Reichquist. "On the contrary. I just wanted to stop by and thank this young man for all the hard work he is putting in. My wife and I were a bit taken aback Sabbath and just wanted to make sure Peter knows he has our support."

"Thank you," I said, dazed. I couldn't believe what was happening. He was the first nonfamily, nonteacher, who appreciated what I was doing.

"No problem. I was also wondering if we couldn't have a special prayer, Ms. Witherspoon, right here—just a quick one." She agreed—just as shocked as I was. Afterward, Mr. Reichquist made his way out and wished us a good day. Because of the interruption, we had run into math time, so the spelling bee was ended without Lucas and I competing. Praise the Lord! God was with me today—especially when our class was interrupted again.

We had managed to complete only one math worksheet when another knock came on our door. This time, the individual wasn't as gracious. It was "Old Man Crabtree," which is what we all call him when our parents aren't around, and he was carrying that wicked cane.

"Mr. Crabtree!" exclaimed Ms. Witherspoon as she opened the door.

"That's right, Educator—it's Crabtree." He barged his way in and surveyed the class until he spotted me and pointed at me with his cane.

"That one there—Peter, is it?" I nodded, gently setting down my pencil and reaching for my compass just in case I had to defend myself. "Well, so we're all dependent on you, are we?" he said, lowering his cane. "It's a shame—far too much pressure for a young man like you. Still, if you apply yourself—you know what that word *apply* means?"

And he proceeded for thirty minutes to tell me not only what the word meant, but how to do it. I would have thanked him if he weren't so boring and if he didn't rap my desk with his cane every time I started to doze off. Several times, Ms. Witherspoon tried to hurry him along, but Mr. Crabtree is old and has earned the right to be stubborn—at least that's what he told us.

When he finally left, it was time for English. But our lesson on verbs had to wait as three more people made their way into the classroom, much to everyone's chagrin. Greetings from well-wishers, prayer warriors, guest lecturers, and those offering pity flooded our classroom. When lunch finally came, everyone was eager to get out of the room and get some peace.

"Well, aren't you Mr. Popular?" said a voice behind me, as I stood in the lunch line. It was Principal Purvis.

"What do you mean?" I asked without looking.

"Mr. Snodgrass tells me that your class has had all sorts of visitors today—is that right?"

"Maybe."

"No need to get defensive," he said, making his way around to face me. He had on his gray suit and a red tie. "You should welcome the support, Peter."

"I suppose it is a change from what usually happens around here," I admitted.

"Indeed, which is why I have let people know that Ms. Witherspoon's fifth-grade class is welcoming visitors—all week—in order to give you a boost. I'm sure your classmates won't mind the attention. Have a good lunch."

The afternoon saw three more visits. The first two were short and not too bad, although every time someone knocks at the door now, I get stares from everybody in class, and Jennifer said we should install one of those "take a number" dispensers they have at the customer service counter in some stores.

The final visit was the worst.

Ms. Witherspoon answered the door, and in walked a man with long hair, a scraggly beard, a leather coat with western-style tassels, and a guitar. My instincts told me to run, but there were too many desks blocking my way to make a clean dash out of the room. The man's name was Echo—at least that's what he told us. I remembered him as a recent convert at last year's evangelistic series. Dad told me he had a good heart but had a bad case of the "sixties." I didn't understand what Dad meant at the time, but now I think it probably has something to do with Echo's name, hair, and the flower stickers all over his guitar.

"I would like to take this opportunity, Ms. Witherspoon," he began dramatically, while raising his right hand and pausing with each phrase for emphasis, "to play a song . . . I have written . . . and dedicated . . . to Peter."

Lucas smiled and applauded; Harley put his head down on his desk so I wouldn't see him laugh; and Ms. Witherspoon grabbed what looked like Tylenol out of her desk, downed a couple pills—and motioned with her hand for Echo to begin the song.

"I call this, 'The Day Peter Saved the School.' " He strummed what I believe was a G chord, signaling the beginning of his tune—and the most awkward moment of my life.

To say his song was an abomination would be a compliment. He looked right at me as he sang, with a voice that came within a few inches of the right note, then stopped and stayed there for prolonged periods of time. It sounded like the type of folk music they sometimes play on NPR—except for the chorus that seemed to have been written by a cheerleader:

Peter, Peter, he's no fool!
Reading, writing, arithmetic—he'll save our school!

Each time Echo sang the chorus, I felt myself breaking out in hives, and I could hear Harley snorting with muffled glee with his head in his arms. I couldn't blame him. The rest of the class was doing the same thing—including Ms. Witherspoon. If I weren't the subject of this humiliation, I would have been right there with them.

After four verses of agonizingly trite lyrics—which no doubt would be quoted *ad nauseam* by every student in the school—the song ended. And a good thing too. I was almost ready to stab myself with my pencil, just to take my mind off the song that I was beginning to think didn't have an end.

The class clapped, whooped, and hollered—and Lucas was the loudest, shouting "Encore! Encore!" Echo bowed low and then walked over to my desk.

"Peter, did you appreciate the song?"

What on earth am I supposed to say to this guy?

"Well, Peter?" said Lucas with a malicious grin.

I wanted to smash his head with Echo's guitar. I had to think fast; I couldn't lie, and I didn't want to confuse the poor man—not more than he already was. I took a deep breath and ventured an answer. "Yes." That wasn't a lie. Granted, I believe that song should never be performed in public again, but after all, it *was* a thoughtful gesture.

"Really?" he said, beaming and tossing his long brown hair over his shoulder. "What did you like about it?"

I didn't even think before I spoke. "The end." A few people laughed quietly to themselves, and Ms. Witherspoon's eyes grew wide. Echo looked puzzled for a second. I held my breath, aware of what I had said.

Then Echo smiled. "That's my favorite part too. God bless you, Peter! And now I must go; I have more classrooms to play!"

"Marvelous," I muttered. I couldn't wait for Mary to hear the song and tell my folks about it over supper.

The last period of the day went quickly, except for an incident in the hallway. I went to get a drink of water, and some eighth-graders on a bathroom break told me that if I failed and the school closed, they would have to be homeschooled. They didn't want to be homeschooled. They made this point clear by making fists and offering to give me a new hairdo via hanging me upside down and dunking my head in the toilet.

"So you'd better not fail us, Peter," said the largest one, poking my chest with his finger. I heartily agreed with them and made my way back to class.

After school, I set up my materials for the tutoring session while listening to the exiting second-graders singing a verse from Echo's song down the hallway.

The school has a smoking crater,
Cheer up, folks, here comes Pay-ter!

I don't know why he felt compelled to rhyme my name with *crater*. I know from my English lessons that he was attempting something called "assonance," which is when you place two words that sound similar next to each other. Unfortunately, when Echo attempted it, he couldn't put two brain cells together, which is why he ended up with a lyrical disaster that will no doubt follow me all the days of my life.

"Sorry, Peter—seems you are at the top of the music charts," said Ms. Witherspoon, sitting next to me.

"Great!"

"Well, look on the bright side—at least you have more support. And I also want to remind you of how well you did today in the spelling and math drills. Your worksheets were one hundred percent. Only Lucas had the other perfect score."

I looked up, unable to contain my smile. "Really? Perfect scores?"

"Quite an improvement over your usual seventy percent, don't you think?"

"Yeah, it is!" I said, feeling the joy of victory washing away the words of my unauthorized theme song. The text from Joshua 1 about God being with us wherever we go drifted through my mind, and I felt like God actually noticed me and was on my side. "Does this mean I don't have to do any more math reviews?"

"No, but it does mean we don't have to do as much."

"Fair enough. So, what's on the agenda this afternoon?"

"Well, I want you to tell me about English grammar. Some of the kids said you were practically speaking another language on the bus this morning, telling them about 'unnecessary clauses.' "

"If we have to, " I complained, opening my English textbook and thinking back to my audio lessons.

"We have to. However, if I am impressed with your progress, I'll let you out an hour early. And I expect to be impressed from what I am seeing and hearing. I've already called your dad to let him know to pick you up early."

"Then, Ms. Witherspoon," I said, sitting up straight, "prepare to be impressed."

* * * *

Before bed, Mom and Dad made their usual round to tuck me in and to pray with me. "Well, in spite of the song, I'm glad you had a good day academically, Son," said Dad, sitting at the foot of my bed.

"Yes, we are *very* proud, Peter; you have really been working hard," agreed Mom, kissing my forehead.

"Ugh—that stupid song! It's stuck in my head. I really wish Mary hadn't regaled us with it at supper."

They laughed. "It *is* pretty awful," said Mom. "But Echo meant well, as you know, and in time the song will fade."

"Yeah, like in seven years when I graduate from high school. Honestly, Mom, this is the sort of thing that's going to be immortalized in the yearbook—and they'll probably make a plaque featuring the lyrics."

"Don't be dramatic, Peter," said Dad. Easy for him to say—he doesn't have to go to school tomorrow. "So, only six days until showtime," he continued. "Do you feel ready?"

"I feel sick."

"It's just nerves, Peter," said Mom, stroking my head.

"Oh really? Just nerves? Great—now I feel better."

"Peter, you know what I mean. I know you're nervous, but you will do fine. Don't let anything convince you otherwise."

"But what if I *don't* do fine?" I said, sitting up. "What if I panic and forget everything in front of all those people? What if I blow it?"

This time Dad put his arm around me. "It doesn't matter, Peter. I've never seen you work this hard at something you didn't want to do. And you have done it for others. I know you think you didn't have a choice, but you didn't have to apply yourself this hard. Whatever happens, you have done well."

"I just hope those eighth-graders feel the same way," I grumbled.

"What eighth-graders?" asked Mom sharply.

"Never mind," I replied, flopping back on my pillow. "I just want this contest to be over with."

"I hear you, sport," said Dad, pulling the blankets over me. "For now, just try to sleep and focus on studies—not what other people say."

"Or sing," I added.

"In any case, let's pray," said Dad. Mom and Dad knelt by my bed, and Dad spoke to God. "Dear Jesus, thank You for bringing Peter this far. Help him not to feel nervous, but to remember what he has studied. Help him to find confidence as he continues to participate in class and prepares to represent Your school. Amen."

Mom left first to make sure Mary was in bed. As Dad was leaving, he stopped and looked at the top of my dresser. The crumpled white piece of paper with the Daniel text on it was still there—untouched from when I put it there.

"Have you had a chance to look this up, Peter?" asked Dad.

"Not yet," I replied, rolling over to face him. "I've got plenty of Bible texts floating around my head. I don't need one more."

Dad gave me a look. "Peter, you can never have too many texts floating around in your head. I'd really like you to take a look at this text."

"I'll get to it."

"OK," said Dad tentatively. "In the meantime, can I borrow it?"

"Sure," I said. "Maybe you should preach on it."

Dad only smiled as he took the crumpled piece of paper in his hand and shut the door.

CHAPTER SEVENTEEN
SIGNS OF INTELLIGENCE

"I believe the answer is Genesis . . .

"Turquoise . . .

"Negative fifty . . .

"Thirty-two degrees . . .

"Jupiter . . .

"Leonardo DaVinci . . .

"Washington D.C. . . ."

"Yes! Correct again, Peter Paul!" exclaimed Ms. Witherspoon, clapping her hands. The rest of the class was stunned—but not as stunned as I was. For the last four class periods, I had been dominating the questions asked in class. I couldn't explain it—the answers just seemed to be there. Dad's extra prayers had finally kicked in after a week. That and the fact that Snotgrass was at a dental appointment until after lunch.

"Wow, Peter! Yesterday, it was spelling and math," said Gretchen, grinning. "Today, its geography, history, Bible, science, *and* English. Did you get that learn-while-you-sleep machine I told you about?"

"No," said Ms. Witherspoon with pride. "Peter has been studying very hard, and it is finally starting to sink in."

"Well, it's about time we started seeing signs of intelligence," said Naomi. "Sunday is the competition—and I was beginning to feel sick."

"You always feel sick, Puke-a-hontas," said Tommy, who sat to her right. Naomi glared at him.

"At least I don't have the coordination of a drunk goose!"

Tommy was about to respond when Ms. Witherspoon stepped between their desks. "Class, let's not ruin this by fighting. We should all be very proud of Peter and focus on supporting him."

"Hear, hear!" agreed Sam. "Why don't we all sing a verse of that song?" Before anyone could stop him, he managed to get out:

His grades are improving, and his mind's gaining power.
Peter's wisdom is like a rare, blossoming flower.

"Three cheers for the blossoming flower," said Principal Purvis, who was standing all of a sudden in the doorway with his creepy nephew. They were both grinning as the class laughed at the flower comment.

"As you can see, Ms. Witherspoon, Lucas is back from the dentist early. His teeth are perfect, as you would expect from our *best* student. Go take your desk, Lucas. And by all means, carry on with the singing—I'm sure it's the best use of the class' time." Ms. Witherspoon didn't seem too happy as Principal Purvis left. The room felt awkward—which Lucas took as an invitation to speak.

"Well, Peter Paul, it appears you have once again done something smart. Two days in a row—how do you manage such an impressive intelligent streak?"

"Simple," I replied before Ms. Witherspoon cut us off and sent us all to lunch. "I follow your example by having no social life."

* * * *

By the time I sat down at the table for lunch, students were buzzing about my performance that morning in class.

"I think he's taking smart pills," offered Naomi. "Peter, answer me honestly—are you on drugs?"

"No."

"Maybe he's a genius, and he has just been bored all this time," suggested Gretchen.

"Could be," I said, smiling.

"No way," insisted Calvin. "Don't you remember what happened on the bus yesterday? That was some of the most boring stuff on the planet."

"Yeah, that's true," admitted Gretchen.

"Maybe he's . . . I mean . . . uh . . . ," said Tommy, getting lost in his own thoughts. "Just give me a sec. It's right there. Um . . . nope—nope, it's gone." I just hope Tommy doesn't work with heavy machinery when he grows up.

"Thanks, Tommy," I replied, giving him credit for making an effort.

"Don't worry," said Harley, taking a bite out of his sandwich. "I think your studying is starting to pay off—like Ms. Witherspoon says." Most of my classmates nodded.

"Oh come on you, guys," complained Lucas, who was sitting at the third-grade table across from us. "It's obvious that Ms. Witherspoon is telling him the questions she is going to ask and giving him the answers to study. It's a ruse to make us think he is smart—but I know the truth."

"And so do all your third-grade friends," I said, earning a laugh from several kids nearby. It felt good, so I continued—oblivious to the figure behind me. "Tell me, Lucas, do you sit with the younger grades because they aren't smart enough yet to recognize the loser you really are?"

"Maybe," said a familiar voice behind me. "Or maybe he just wants to be a good academic influence on them, instead of basking in his own short-lived popularity."

Principal Purvis! Why is he always in the lunchroom? I haven't been able to eat a meal in peace for weeks. He put his heavy hand on my shoulder, letting me feel his weight. *Maybe he gets free food, and that's why he's always here.*

"I caution you, Peter. Be more respectful of your fellow students, or I'll make sure you have detention even *after* the contest—do you understand?" All eyes were on me, and it made my face red and hot. It wouldn't do any good to make a smart remark here.

"Yes, sir."

"Good! Now, as an act of goodwill, why don't you offer to take Lucas's tray to the trash for him? That's a good boy."

As I took Lucas's tray to the trash, a chorus of third-graders began to sing another verse of Echo's song as they lined up for recess.

Peter seems to have all the answers; he's been studying, you see,
But don't be duped,
And don't be fooled.
It's the Witherspoon-Pappenfuss conspiracy!

Echo didn't write that verse, but I can guess who did.

* * * *

I didn't answer any more questions as the classes dragged by—but Lucas did. I just watched him get one right answer after another. Some people looked at me funny, and I did my best not to meet their gaze. I actually knew some of the answers, but I just didn't feel up to it. If I got the answers right, it would just invite more garbage from Snotgrass. Unfortunately, because I didn't answer any questions in the afternoon, I could hear kids murmuring—after school was out and they began making their way to the lobby—that the Witherspoon-Pappenfuss conspiracy might actually be true and that she was telling me the questions and answers in advance.

I slouched at my desk and tilted my head back to look at the ceiling. "The day started so well . . . ," I said to myself. Ms. Witherspoon heard me.

"I'm sorry, Peter. I'm frustrated too." I looked up to see her close the classroom door and then make her way to the desk in front of me. "It seems we're fighting an uphill battle."

"A very steep hill," I agreed.

"But at least we're fighting," she continued. "And you have quite a bit of fight in you."

"Too bad Mr. Purvis and Snotgrass have more."

"I know," she said, ignoring my "Snotgrass" remark. "I've been thinking about that and the situation that Lucas and Mr. Purvis are in. They seem determined to ruin the chance they feel you took from them."

"No kidding!" I said, crossing my arms and letting the thought of their actions fester in my mind. "I wish there was something we could do."

"Maybe there is," said Ms. Witherspoon, looking right at me. "I've been thinking—especially in light of this newfound conspiracy theory—that maybe what we need is to have a friendly competition to allow Principal Purvis and Lucas to prove their point."

"What?"

"Sure. We could allow Principal Purvis to select the questions and emcee the event. And we could arrange it so that you and Lucas go head-to-head—this Friday, before school is out." Clearly, the woman had lost her marbles.

"Ms. Witherspoon, how much Tylenol have you had today?"

She laughed and shook her head. "None—and I don't think this is a bad idea. Think about it. You would get acquainted with the kind of pressure you'll be facing on Sunday—even without Lucas competing—and it would give the school a chance to see that you really have done your homework for once."

I groaned.

Ms. Witherspoon put her hand on mine. "Peter, I think this is important for you and the school—and as your tutor, I am making this your final lesson."

My stomach was doing backflips. "You really think this is a good idea?"

"I do."

She gripped my hand tightly, and her eyes sparkled with determination. Her confidence began to soothe my sickly stomach. I nodded hesitantly.

"If you say so, but I guess that means there is no getting out of tutoring early for the rest of the week, is there?"

"I'm afraid not."

"OK," I sighed, "let's do it."

"Great! We'll do a quick review of all subjects, then do some drills." She went to her desk and pulled out her tutoring materials—all of them. I felt another sensation that prompted me to ask another question.

"Ms. Witherspoon?"

"Yes, Peter?"

"Do you have any more Tylenol?"

* * * *

There were gasps when the contest announcement was made over the school intercom. Principal Purvis was so taken with the idea that not only did he begin referring to Ms. Witherspoon as his "favorite teacher," he blocked out the last hour on Friday so the entire school could watch Lucas and me compete in the gymnasium.

Reactions varied when people came to their senses. Gretchen said she would be praying three times a day for me. Harley suspected Ms. Witherspoon had caved under the stress and was double-crossing me to get in good with Principal Purvis. And Lucas was absolutely giddy. He walked right up to my desk after the announcement and extended a hand.

"May the best scholar win," he said sweetly. When I reached out to shake his hand, he jerked it away. I had fallen for the oldest trick in the book. "Let's hope your brain is faster than your hands, Pappenfuss." The class responded with the inevitable *"Ooooooooooooooh,"* before Ms. Witherspoon broke it up.

"Alright, Lucas, go back to your seat," she told him. "And I expect better sportsmanship on Friday—is that clear?"

"Yes, Teacher," he said, faking innocence. "I apologize for my behavior." Ms. Witherspoon didn't respond, which made me feel a little better.

"OK, class, let's get ready for math."

While Ms. Witherspoon was giving instructions, I received a note from across the room. I opened it and read,

Lucas is just scared of you. Good luck, Peter. We believe in you.

It was followed by six signatures: Harley, Gretchen, Melissa, Sam, and Wesley. Half the class. *So, they're split down the middle.* Then I realized that neither my signature nor Lucas's would be on the note, of course, so that left a total of eleven—which meant I had the majority on my side. I smiled as I folded the note back up and put it in my pocket. Several pairs of eyes looked at me, and I smiled in acknowledgment of their support. I had two days before the pre-contest to bolster my support. I was ready, and I raised my hand when Ms. Witherspoon asked the first question of the period—and gave the right answer!

* * * *

Wednesday and Thursday flew by quickly as Ms. Witherspoon and I studied our brains out after school. I had been getting all A's on my homework, and my parents—as expected—are thrilled. My tutoring sessions really feel like a team effort, and Ms. Witherspoon assured me she is on my side. This week, I even got all correct answers in class, beating out Lucas twice in a row in science with my swift hand raising.

"Looks like his reflexes have improved since Monday," commented Chandra, who came up to me at recess and said she wanted her name added to the list of signatures on Tuesday's note. Snotgrass—as you can imagine—has been living up to his nickname.

He has been deliberately walking past my desk, whispering things like "Loser," "Cheater," "Failure," and "Stupid." If that weren't enough, every time he raises his hand and gets an answer right in class, he'll say things like "Did Peter's hand even twitch on that one?" or "Maybe Peter hasn't studied that yet—he'd better hurry up." Once Ms. Witherspoon sent him to the principal's office. But when he came back with a chocolate bar, she abandoned that punishment.

I told Dad about it Thursday night before the contest while we shared a snack of fudge brownies and milk. Even though it was health food night, Mom made them as a special treat because of my improved performance.

"I think Principal Purvis should get a 'pastoral visit,'" I suggested to Dad. "Maybe the church board should take a look at his membership."

"Peter, you shouldn't say things like that," Dad scolded. "I'm not visiting him, but I will call him tonight and have a chat; it isn't right for students being punished to get chocolate. I know you're aggravated, but I've told you that Principal Purvis and his nephew have their own issues to deal with and it's best to focus on your goals and the task at hand. Besides," he said, pointing to the refrigerator, which was completely covered with A papers belonging to me, "you have quite a bit to be happy about."

"You can't even see my art projects," complained Mary, walking into the room in her pink Hello Kitty pajamas. She wore a scowl as she stood next to the fridge, lifting paper after paper in search of her drawings.

"Now, honey, your mom and I love your artwork, but you've had the spotlight for a long time. It's Peter's turn for a little while—OK?" She wasn't listening, as she continued to flip desperately through the pages until she came upon one of her drawings. She had done it with colored pencils. Yellows, browns, and black adorned the page in miscellaneous shapes.

"It looks like those crop circles that aliens make," I commented.

"It's a giraffe," she hissed.

"Yes, and it's a lovely giraffe, *isn't* it, Peter?" said Dad.

I shrugged. "If that's what you want to believe, Dad—you go right ahead. But just to be safe, we should leave them covered up."

"So what you're saying," said Dad, "is that it's time for bed?"

"I think that's exactly what he's saying," agreed Mary. "He has the pre-contest tomorrow, and unless he gets eight hours of sleep, he'll be even crankier than he is now."

"She's right, Peter. You need your rest—we all do."

Dad ushered us both up to our rooms. After prayers, I lay in my room staring at the ceiling, doing my best to fall asleep. I couldn't. My mind wouldn't stop thinking about tomorrow. I got up and went to the window to look out at the street. It was nine o'clock, and there wasn't much activity. The moon was full, and I stared at it for a while before kneeling down and praying until I fell asleep.

CHAPTER EIGHTEEN
THE PRE-CONTEST

Mom came into my room after calling me three times for breakfast, and found me asleep on the floor by my window. She made me eat breakfast. I wanted to sleep—at least until noon after the pre-contest.

"Just tell them I'm sick and that it isn't safe for me to leave the toilet."

"Peter, you need a good breakfast so you'll have the strength to do your best. Now get dressed and come downstairs. Don't worry about missing the bus; I'm taking you to school this morning."

The morning was a blur until PE when we played dodgeball. I was doing my best to pay attention as balls whizzed past me. Harley grabbed a ball and came to my side.

"Come on, Pete—get it together! You've been a zombie all morning, and although that may keep you alive in history class, it's not going to work here!" He threw a ball at Naomi who was staring into space—and nailed her right in the knees, nearly knocking her over. Harley's point was well taken. But I still wasn't myself. I couldn't concentrate on anything but my upcoming doom at eleven o'clock. Then Lucas started in.

Snotgrass had been horrible all morning. When Ms. Witherspoon left the room, he called me a chicken in front of everyone, because I was late to school. To make matters worse, Mr. Purvis met me before I got to class and said if I misbehaved at all, Lucas would be declared the winner by default on account of my lack of sportsmanship. So for two hours I had to take every snide comment, every rude gesture, and every insult Lucas hurled at me—while the class looked on, not sure whether getting involved would help me.

Now Lucas came sauntering up to the dodgeball line with a nasty grin. His glasses were freshly polished, his curly hair was trim and neat, and he was wearing slacks and a dress shirt—no doubt dressed for his inevitable success.

"You're looking a little sick, Peter. Maybe you should have stayed home." I tried to ignore him, but he continued. "You're going to have to speak up a little more if you intend to compete *at all* today." I looked at him and the smug look on his face as our classmates ran around us with rubber balls flying through the air. I was exhausted and just wanted the day to be over.

"Lucas, can you please just leave me alone today? I'm not in the mood." He laughed and then began mocking me with a baby voice.

"Aww, is wittle Petey scawed?" I could feel my blood pressure rising with each mispronounced word as he continued his taunts. *Where is Ms. Witherspoon?* I looked, and she was busy talking to Wesley who *always* tried to get out of playing anything. Unless someone started crying, she wouldn't look up until Wesley was finished whining—and I wasn't going to give Lucas that kind of satisfaction. I tried to move down the line, but he followed.

"Awr woo twying to wun away, Peetey? Aw, poh Peetey." Some of my classmates were looking at Lucas now as he continued his baby talk; a few people told him to knock it off, but he ignored them.

I resolved to move back toward the "jail" area so he couldn't talk to me as easily, but he got right in my line of vision and started making faces. I know it wasn't a big deal, but with every face I felt myself getting angrier. With every gesture, I felt my fists clench tighter and tighter. With every moment that Lucas Snodgrass's obnoxious behavior went unchecked, I felt myself resolve to give him the pounding of his life. *Who cares if I lose today? Sunday is the real contest, anyway.*

I locked my gaze on Lucas and began to walk directly toward him. Harley saw me and shouted at me to stop. I ignored him. Ms. Witherspoon didn't look up, figuring that Harley's yelling was related to the dodgeball game. Snotgrass smiled at me as I approached.

"Well, Pappenfuss," he said coolly, dropping the baby talk, "what are you going to do?" I couldn't think of anything to say. I just clenched and un-clenched my fists—relishing how good it would feel to slug him square in the nose. However, there was a thin line of rational thought screaming at me in the back of my mind, telling me to walk away. Lucas capitalized on my moment of indecision.

"I see you're slower than usual. Here, let me help you." He thrust out his chin and closed his eyes. Out of the corner of my eye I could see Harley talk-ing to Ms. Witherspoon. She looked up and immediately blew her whistle and began making her way toward us, but the game continued—and so did our confrontation. Lucas saw the same thing I did and placed his hands behind his back and extended his face right over the line.

"Come on, sweetheart," he urged, "time's up. Ms. Witherspoon is com-ing, so why don't you hurry up—unless you're afraid that your fist is as weak as your mind. Poor wittle Peetey hits wike a giwl . . . a wittle giwl."

I cocked my fist and readied my punch, when out of the blue I felt a whoosh of air fly by my head. It was a ball—a large rubber dodgeball moving at the speed of light. The air sizzled in its wake. And the beauty of it was that since Lucas's eyes were closed, he didn't see it coming!

WHAM! WHOMP!

The sound resonated around the gym. The impact threw Lucas's head back and spun him around. Before he could cry out in pain, another speeding ball flew straight into his gut—*THUNK*—doubling him over and taking his breath away. He stood there for a moment in a semisquat, eyes wide, face contorted, bearing the imprint of the ball on the right side of his face—before falling over to writhe in pain at my feet.

"I've had all I can stand of that kid," said Calvin, coming up behind me.

"Nice shot!" I said, awestruck.

Calvin shrugged. "It wasn't too hard—he has a big head."

"No kidding," said Jennifer from the other side of the line.

"You hit your own teammate?" I asked incredulously, while Lucas con-tinued to roll around, moaning, at our feet.

"Yeah. Well, he wasn't participating, anyway."

"What on earth has gotten into you two?" said Ms. Witherspoon, hurrying up and helping the sniveling Snodgrass to his feet and escorting him to the sidelines. Naomi was commissioned to fetch Principal Purvis, and it wasn't long before he burst red-faced into the gym.

"You realize you are both getting detention for this?" I said to Calvin and Jennifer.

"Then you had better make it worth it—and win," said Jennifer, just as Mr. Purvis came over and escorted them to his office.

* * * *

Calvin and Jennifer were sentenced to a week's detention but were still allowed to attend the pre-contest. The bad news was that Lucas spent the rest of the day with the school nurse and was expected to recover from his injuries in time to compete. When classes were finally dismissed and we went to the gym, we all got our first look at him since PE.

He was standing on the stage with his usual sour expression, but augmenting it was a huge red mark on the side of his face. You could still see the texture of the ball. His lower lip was a little swollen, and he wasn't standing totally straight. Personally, I think the dodgeballs had improved his looks.

So did Harley. "Nice birthmark, Lucas. Have you always had it or is that something the dentist did to you this morning?" Lucas glared at him, which made Harley even more delighted. "Well, at least you haven't lost your sweet disposition."

"Leave him alone, Harley," I said as we took our seats. "He's had enough."

While the classes were filtering in, Ms. Witherspoon asked me to meet her in one of the rooms on the side of the stage. She wanted to give me a pep talk. "Peter," she began, "you know just as much as Lucas, and even if you falter—just view this as practice. The real competition is on Sunday."

"That's what I told myself when I was about to punch Lucas in the face and risk losing by default."

"Well, thank goodness someone else beat you to it." I raised my eyebrows.

"You're thankful Lucas got hit with the dodgeballs?"

"Peter, I never condone violence. Sometimes, however, the school of hard knocks is the best way to learn a lesson."

"Oh, I agree," I said, smiling. "If you want, I could arrange hard knocks to be part of his curriculum from here on."

"Don't push it, Peter! Now, let's pray and get back out there."

* * * *

There were a few courtesy competitors before Snodgrass and I were called up to begin the real match. We took our places on either side of the podium and faced our fellow classmates. They were silent, and I think I saw some eighth-grade boys taking bets unbeknownst to their teacher.

Principal Purvis was in his element. "And now the moment we have all been waiting for," he announced, "the chance to see if Peter's tutoring with my favorite teacher—Ms. Witherspoon—will be enough to give us victory on Sunday. Now, you boys know the rules. You each have a flashlight. The first person to turn on his flashlight and answer the question gets a point. We will play to twenty points. Ready?"

Lucas looked at me and scowled. I wasn't fazed. That glowing red mark on his face took all the edge out of his nastiness. "I'm ready," I said calmly—winking at Lucas. He gritted his teeth.

"I'm more than ready," he hissed—much to the delight of the student body.

"I have no doubts, Lucas. I have no doubts," said Principal Purvis. They shared a knowing look, and it dawned on me that they could have a conspiracy of their own. *What if they had gotten together and worked out the questions and answers?* It didn't matter. Ms. Witherspoon was right; Sunday was the real competition. I relaxed and took a deep breath as Principal Purvis read the first question.

"Tell me," he said looking at Lucas as if he expected him to answer before me, "what is the capital of North Dakota?"

Lucas swiftly turned on his flashlight, but it was followed by Harley's voice. "Peter's light was on first!" Several people clapped. The principal turned around and scrutinized me—and then the rest of the students. Students—and even some of the teachers—were nodding in agreement with Harley.

Mr. Purvis raised an eyebrow. "Very well, Pappenfuss—what do you think the answer is?"

"And it has to be a *real* city," added Lucas. Mr. Purvis didn't say anything but waited along with the rest of the school for my answer.

I cleared my throat. "Bismarck."

There was applause from the student body and a stunned look on Lucas's face. I had drawn first blood. Principal Purvis looked surprised, too, before acknowledging the answer. "Correct," he said—but he didn't sound too pleased about it. More applause. My idiot friend Harley got everyone to sing the bridge from Echo's song:

Go, Peter, go!
Know, Peter, know!

I am beginning to hate this song more than health food night, Harold Crosby's lectures, and Mary's dumb friends combined. Principal Purvis ended the chanting by raising his hand sharply and continuing the contest. "The score is one to nothing. Next question." He straightened himself up and shot a look at Lucas, who was still trying to compose himself.

"It must be the head injury I sustained," he said apologetically.

"Next time move out of the way," said his uncle, sharply annoyed. "After all, isn't that the basic idea of dodgeball?"

"Let's hope the next question isn't on physical education," called out an unidentified student, which made everyone laugh.

"Everyone needs to be quiet!" Mr. Purvis commanded. "OK, on to question number two. What is the top speed of a cheetah?"

This time Lucas was first. "Seventy miles per hour, but only over short distances." Mr. Purvis smiled widely and patted his nephew on the shoulder, while everyone else groaned.

"Very good, Lucas. And as for you groaners, I think Lucas should get applause as well—it's only fair." There was some haphazard clapping but nothing special. Ms. Witherspoon winked at me, and I understood. Except for Lucas and his uncle, everyone was cheering for me. I felt renewed strength and smiled.

"Pappenfuss, why are you grinning like that?" demanded Mr. Purvis. "*You* didn't answer the question."

"That's right," I said, not looking at him, "but the score is only one to one. I have time." With that, he continued the contest, and to the elation of my classmates, I answered the next three questions correctly. Lucas got the following question, but then I responded by getting another three. It was an incredible rush—being able to field questions—and I began to appreciate why Lucas studied so hard. *I wonder if he feels this way all the time.*

"What's the score?" I asked pleasantly, as the flustered principal frantically shuffled his question cards.

"Six to two, Pappenfuss," he snapped and moved ahead with the next question. Lucas got it—because I let him. It wasn't because I'm arrogant but because I felt bad for him. He looked shell-shocked, and I began to wonder if maybe Calvin's ball had hit him in the head *too* hard. He didn't even have the presence of mind to make nasty faces at me. He was honestly trying to compete, but he didn't really expect me to know anything. And whenever he did get a correct answer, he received only weak applause, which couldn't help matters. I let him get the next question, as well.

"Well," said Mr. Purvis, mopping his forehead with his handkerchief, "it looks like Lucas is gaining." Lucas smiled a little and nodded. "Six to four, everyone, six to four. Perhaps Pappenfuss has realized exactly who he is dealing with, and now it will take every brain cell he has to hang on to his meager lead!"

A really awkward feeling spread through the room. I think right at that moment, it dawned on *everybody* that Principal Purvis was—and had been—playing favorites and hadn't been treating me fairly. As a teacher, his responsibility was to help every student do well—not just those related to him. He could sense the awkwardness, too, and I noticed he looked embarrassed.

I looked at Ms. Witherspoon who was smiling at me with soft eyes. She had worked so hard. I saw Mary, but she refused to acknowledge my presence—preferring to giggle with her friends instead of participating in the awkward moment involving her brother. I looked at my classmates, who were staring blankly at me—except Harley. Harley narrowed his eyes, looked as serious as he could, and nodded for me to finish this. I narrowed my eyes and nodded back, taking one last glance at Ms. Witherspoon and giving her a smile. She gave me a puzzled look. She had no idea what I was up to.

"Let's have the next question," I said in a steely tone, and Mr. Purvis quickly complied, wanting the awkward moment to end.

"How far away is the sun from planet Earth?"

"Ninety-three million miles," I responded quickly.

Seven to four.

"When did America declare its independence?"

"1776."

Eight to four.

Mr. Purvis was getting nervous and took off his suit coat. Lucas, meanwhile, smacked his flashlight on the podium. "I think it's broken," he complained.

"It will be—if you keep doing that!" hissed his uncle, continuing the questions that were beginning to feel more like an interrogation of my intelligence than a contest. The competition continued with Principal Purvis growing louder and louder and the questions coming faster and faster—so fast that I think Lucas gave up after I reached fifteen correct answers. Mr. Purvis was looking at me straight in the eye as he rattled off his queries. His eyes flashed, and his face turned red, but I held my ground.

"What is photosynthesis?"

"The conversion of light energy into chemical energy by living organisms!"

"What was Mark Twain's real name?"

"Samuel Clemens!"

"Finish the grammatical rule: *I* before *e* except after . . . ?"

"C!"

"SPELL *BANANA*!"

"B-A-N-A-N-A!"

"WINNER! W-I-N-N-E-R!" I shouted, my hands trembling and my legs shaking with adrenaline. "Unless you want to play to thirty points!"

The school erupted with applause, and Mr. Purvis slammed down his cards. Mary sat in wide-eyed disbelief. Ms. Witherspoon rushed up front to hug me. Harley and Gretchen followed with high fives and "congratulations," and Sam Feltzer leaped onto his chair and did his usual happy dance—resulting in a happy fall into the seventh-grade girls sitting behind him.

"Peter, I am so proud of you," said Ms. Witherspoon. "How do you feel?"

"Good—I guess." I was still trying to grasp what had happened. *I had actually won!*

"You guess?" said Harley amazed. "You just blew away the principal's nephew—and you *guess* you feel good?"

"Did I really beat him that bad?"

"The score was twenty to four, Peter," said Harley, grinning. "That makes you five times smarter than Lucas. Hey, everyone, my best friend is a genius!"

"I dunno," I said, "I feel kind of funny. It was sort of intense at the end."

"You're right, Peter. It did get a little exciting," agreed Ms. Witherspoon. "But let's not dwell on that." She ushered us all back to class where we were officially dismissed for the weekend. She said that because my performance was so good, I was to put in only an hour of study at home and not to worry about tutoring. It would be nice to enjoy a weekend for once.

Dad was waiting outside and gave me a huge hug and clapped me on the shoulder. "Your mom and I heard about what happened today. We're so excited for you, Peter."

I was excited, too, although I couldn't shake a nagging, uneasy feeling over the way Mr. Purvis had acted. Dad noticed that something was on my mind.

"I also heard about what happened with Mr. Purvis. I want you to know that there is a meeting at three o'clock this afternoon, and I hope that from now on, things won't escalate like they did today." I nodded and made my way to the car—but not before Lacey Cromwell dashed out the front door of the school and caught up with us.

"Pastor Pappenfuss, wait! WAIT!" she cried. When she reached us, Lacey eyed me up and down and shook her head.

"Peter."

"Yes?"

"I'm impressed with the sharpness of your mind, but your wardrobe is not going to pass on Sunday." She looked at my dad. "Pastor Pappenfuss?"

"Yes, Lacey?"

"Can I have permission to be your son's wardrobe consultant for Sunday?"

Dad laughed. "I think you may have to fight Mrs. Pappenfuss for that job."

"Has she been the one letting Peter pick out his own clothes?"

"Hey, now," I protested, "I do just fine!"

"Um, hello? Brown belt with black shoes? And don't get me started on those jeans, which I know for a fact have been worn three times this week. Won't you let me help him, Mr. Pappenfuss?"

"She does have a point, Peter, and a little more help never hurts. OK, Lacey, you can help. Just let us know what you have in mind. Mrs. Pappenfuss is going shopping this afternoon for a new outfit, and . . ."

"Oh, I already called my parents, and they said I could come."

Dad nodded.

"Thanks!" chirped Lacey, running to her ride.

"Do I *have* to go, Dad?"

"I'm afraid so, Peter. You need to be there to try things on."

When we got in the car, Mary was in her usual spot in the backseat.

"Having wardrobe malfunctions, Peter?" she inquired.

I was going to respond with a malfunction that involved my fist and her arm, but Dad cut me off. "Mary, leave your brother alone—and have you congratulated him yet?"

Mary looked more stunned than she had when I won the pre-contest. "Why *no*, Dad," I said, feigning surprise. "Come to think of it, she hasn't."

"Mary, tell your brother you're proud of him." Mary stumbled over the words before turning to look out the window in disbelief, as Dad started the car and began the drive home.

"Dad?"

"Yes, Peter?"

"I love you."

CHAPTER NINETEEN
THE DAY BEFORE

"Last week, one of you kindly gave my son a Bible text to encourage him as he studied for the contest that is happening tomorrow. The text is Daniel chapter three, verses seventeen and eighteen. It records the words of three young Hebrew men to the king of Babylon: ' "If that is the case, our God whom we serve is able to deliver us from the burning fiery furnace, and He will deliver us from your hand, O king. But if not, let it be known to you, O king, that we do not serve your gods, nor will we worship the gold image which you have set up." '

"Think about it. These young men found themselves in the midst of a fiery trial that threatened their lives—yet they took a stand. They trusted God so much that even if He didn't save them from the fire that day, they knew He was still in control, and it didn't matter. Tomorrow, a young man will face a trial—a trial that could play a role in determining the life of our school. But even if he doesn't win the competition," said Dad, pointing at me, "and even if *He* plans things otherwise," he said, pointing up toward God, "we will still continue to trust and worship Him, because He is in control, and He will provide a way for us to serve Him—Amen?"

The congregation all said "Amen" and looked at me, grinning while they did it. I was on the platform, because Dad had asked me to read the text before he preached. I had never done anything like that before, and for a moment, I felt like Naomi—ready to vomit at the drop of a hat out of nerves.

It was also hard concentrating on Dad's sermon, because Harley kept making faces at me. Once his mom caught him. She grabbed him by his arm and led him out of the sanctuary to have a talk—which I thought was funnier than any of his faces.

It's sort of fun in a weird way, sitting on the platform. You can tell what everyone's doing. I saw three adults pick their noses, two people fall asleep, and one kid take off under the pews with his mother trying to follow him to get him back in his seat. I don't know how Dad keeps from losing his focus. Then there are the people who sit with their arms crossed, scowling, the people who have to use the bathroom every five minutes, and of course, the teenagers in the balcony, pretending to pay attention—but you can totally see them playing on their cell phones.

"At this time," said Dad, closing his Bible on the pulpit, "I would like to recognize the teacher who has worked so hard to tutor our academic champion. Ms. Witherspoon, would you come to the front?" She was wearing a light blue dress with silvery shoes. She smiled at me as she walked up the center aisle and stepped up on the podium.

"Thank you, Pastor. It has been a wonderful opportunity for me to teach at our school this year, and although it's been difficult at times, adding tutoring to my list of duties has been rewarding. As some of you may have heard, we had a pre-contest at school yesterday in which Peter competed against his fellow students. Our principal asked some very difficult questions." There were a few giggles from kids in the congregation and a few nervous-looking adults, but Ms. Witherspoon continued.

"I'm proud to say that not only did Peter win, but he didn't falter on any of the questions." Another corporate "Amen" and a few timid claps made their way around the church. "I firmly believe he is ready for tomorrow and that he stands as good a chance as anyone to win. But as our pastor said, even if he doesn't, God has blessed us so much as a church, and He will lead us through this difficulty in some other way." There were more "Amens," and then she sat down. Dad motioned for me to stand beside him and then asked for one more final prayer for me. This time, people practically leaped to their feet and made their way to the front.

Mom reached me first and gave me a big hug, then knelt beside me with

Dad on the other side. Mary was there as well, putting her hand in Mom's while closing her eyes. But my guess is that she wasn't praying—just trying to avoid looking at me. Everyone else crowded around—young, old, and in-between. Harley and his mom were among the last up on the platform. Harley walked in front of his mom and rolled his eyes so I could see—and so she couldn't.

The prayer was relatively short, but it involved a long pause in the middle so people could spend a few moments praying silently for me. I could really feel the weight of everyone's hands—as well as their prayers, I think—as we all knelt there. Afterward, we had the usual dismissal with me greeting people at the door with Dad. The first people to come out were some eighth-graders from the balcony—including the boys who had threatened me at school with a new hairdo.

However, they were led by Allison Marie Swenson—the most beautiful girl on the planet—or at least in our school. Her long, jet-black hair shimmered as she flicked it over her shoulders. She wore a dark green dress with spaghetti straps that accented her sparkling green eyes. She was also the only girl in school who knew how to wear makeup properly. A few other girls tried, but they always looked like circus clowns. Every boy in school is in love with Allison, and she was the first one out of church.

I had never actually spoken to her—just stared at her from across the gym like everyone else. I felt tingly in my spine and queasy in my stomach. I felt my pupils dilate and my mouth grow dry. A stupid grin I couldn't control swept across my face. My palms also decided to sweat—making them nice and slippery.

"Good morning, Allison," said Dad. "How are you?"

"Very well, Pastor Pappenfuss. And you?" She was so polite—it drove me wild.

"Oh, I'm fine, thank you."

Then Allison turned to me! I couldn't stop my mouth from smiling or my palms from sweating. "Peter," she said. I felt my heart stop.

"Ngah?" I mumbled—which is clearly not a word. She smiled at me in spite of my inability to function like a normal person.

"I'll be praying for your success tomorrow. You'll let me know how it goes, right?"

She's actually talking to me! This time I moved my mouth, but nothing came out—apparently, the part of my brain responsible for speech had become disconnected. However, my right hand extended itself for a handshake. Why it did this, I have no idea. Allison smiled and grabbed my hand in response.

I couldn't wait to feel her touch—to hold hands with her! But my hands were wet. My hand slipped right out of hers like a wet fish. What's worse was that she thought it was her fault—so she tried again.

"Oops!" she said. "Looks like you're a little sweaty there."

"Ngah," I repeated, downheartedly looking at my shoes. She looked at me with a mischievous smile. It was painfully obvious I was nervous. What was worse was that the eighth-grade boys and my own father were witnessing me crash and burn in a pile of sweaty palms and some word my brain had made up all on its own. I wanted her to move on or at least move out of the way, so I could run to the parking lot and lock myself in the car. Instead she lingered, looked at my dad, and then back at me. Then she spoke.

"I know you must be nervous about tomorrow, Peter. Don't be. I have faith in you." I looked up, and she leaned forward, putting her lips on my cheek and setting my face ablaze! Then she winked at me and made her way out to the parking lot.

The next thing I knew, I was swarmed by eighth-grade boys shaking my sweaty hands profusely, patting me on the back, and calling me the "ladies' man."

"Peter, you are now the coolest person I know," said one.

"Yeah, don't worry about tomorrow. I couldn't dunk a man in the toilet who has moves like you do."

"Hear! Hear!" shouted two other eighth-graders.

"Alright, you guys, have a happy Sabbath, and we'll see you around," said Dad, moving them along.

The rest of the line was a blur of compliments and affirmations. I couldn't focus on anything but the kiss until later that afternoon just before sundown.

"*Peter,* I'm not going to ask you again," scolded Mom as we gathered for family worship. "Wipe off that kiss!"

"No way," I replied, covering my cheek. "Allison's love for me will live on through eternity!"

"Peter, this is ridiculous! Walter, come tell your son to wipe the lipstick off his cheek! He's been googly-eyed and moony-faced for five hours now, and I'm getting concerned."

"It's still there?" asked Dad with a smile, coming down the stairs. "She must have been wearing the long-lasting stuff."

"Walter!"

"OK, OK! Your mom is right, Peter. Time to clean up before worship."

"But it's a good luck charm," I protested.

"Charms are for witches, Peter," said Mary, who was sitting next to Mom on the couch.

"*You* would know," I replied, making a face.

"Peter, I know I did not just hear you suggest that your sister is a witch, because if you did—"

"I was just commenting on her intelligence, Mom—which is strangely exceptional for a *human* girl her age."

"You had also better not be suggesting again that she is an alien!"

"All I'm trying to do is tell you people that this token of love on my cheek is a source of strength."

"She doesn't *love* you, Peter; she just felt sorry for you and those sweat machines you call hands," snorted Mary.

"Perhaps you'd like a closer look at my hands, Mary."

"Perhaps you'd both like a closer look at mine," said Dad, standing now in the middle of the living room with his hands on his hips. We both ended our argument but continued to stare daggers at each other.

"Now, Peter," continued Dad, "your mother asked you to wash your cheek, and you need to do it. I'm sure it won't be the last time you're kissed by a girl."

I stood up and sighed. "It might be the last time someone as lovely as Allison kisses me. Who knows what kind of woman I'll have to settle for now, thanks to you people."

"I'm sure with years of therapy, you will survive," said Dad. "Now get to it."

I made my way up the bathroom and washed my face with a heavy heart and made my way back downstairs for family worship. Afterward, Dad announced that he was taking us all out for pizza and that the O'Briens and Ms. Witherspoon would be coming along as a sort of mini-pep rally to give me a boost.

"Did you invite, Allison?" I asked.

"No, Peter," said Dad. "I think one kiss before the contest will be enough."

The rest of the evening was a lot of fun. We went to Pizza Hut and ordered the buffet. I beat Harley by eating seven slices of pizza (he only managed five), and Harley entertained everybody when he laughed so hard his root beer came out his nose, spilled onto the floor, and caused our waitress to slip and dump a plate of spaghetti in Mary's lap. All in all, a most satisfying evening.

That night, as I lay in bed, I felt hopeful. Sabbath had been wonderful, and everyone had been so supportive. I reviewed a few Bible promises in my head and remembered that I had agreed to meet Ms. Witherspoon in the morning at nine o'clock at the school to review some things. The contest started at two o'clock in the afternoon at the Radisson Hotel Ballroom downtown. By supper tomorrow evening, it would be all over, and I would know my fate . . . and the school's.

CHAPTER TWENTY
OCTOBER 22

"Peter, would you hold *still*? I can't fix your tie when you're fidgeting!" Lacey had been working on me for twenty minutes. First, it was the color of my shirt. On Friday, Mom and Lacey managed to pick out three shirts for me: blue, white, and pinstripe. Apparently, blue and white weren't the right colors. Then it was the pants: khaki or black? Following the selection of khakis, we went through seven ties! Mom and Lacey went back and forth so many times changing my appearance that I'm ready to go to this contest naked if it will get me out of another clothes change.

"Let me try, Lacey," said Mom, taking over. Lacey was flushed and flustered and flopped down on the couch in our living room. "There you go, Peter. I think that's the best combination. Walter, how does he look?"

"Well," said Mary before Dad could speak, "his clothes are nice, and you managed to fix his cowlick, but who knows what kind of a mess his brain is in."

"Mary, the Bible says that we have the mind of Christ—Second Corinthians chapter two, verse sixteen. I'm not worried." My recitation caused Mary to narrow her eyes, get off the couch, and approach me.

"The Bible also says that pride goes before destruction, Peter. That's Proverbs chapter sixteen, verse eighteen." She smirked at me, and I could clearly see it was a challenge. Mary had sat by idly for most of the past few weeks, watching me receive the academic attention she was used to. Now her jealousy was clear, and she wanted to make sure I knew she was still the star. However, I had gone to bed for weeks, listening to memory verses, and I was happy to accept her challenge.

"Indeed it does, Mary," I responded in the most pious voice I could muster. "However, I believe it was the apostle Paul who wrote that God's grace is sufficient—Second Corinthians chapter twelve, verse nine."

"Not if you tempt the Lord—Matthew chapter four, verse seven," she responded smugly, crossing her arms.

"Now, children," began Mom, but Dad held up his hand.

"No, no! This . . . this is incredible! Let them finish." Mom stood stunned at Dad's fascination with our scriptural battle.

"Are you accusing me of something, Mary? Revelation chapter twelve, verse ten, says it's the devil who is the accuser of the brethren, and we all know that the devil is cast into the lake of fire in Revelation chapter twenty, verse ten."

"I am merely speaking the truth in love—Ephesians chapter four, verse fifteen, and it's the truth that will set you free, according to John chapter eight, verse thirty-two."

"She's got you there, Pete," said Dad with a grin. I grinned back, enjoying the banter. Mom was still unimpressed.

"Oh, she would, Dad," I retorted, "if it wasn't for First John chapter three, verse eighteen, telling me that it's what we *do* in love and not just what we *say* that makes up the truth, and Mary's body language reminds me more of the hypocrite that destroys his neighbor with his mouth—or *her* mouth, in Mary's case—Proverbs chapter eleven, verse nine."

Mary stamped her foot and growled before she replied. "Peter, your righteousness is like filthy rags—Isaiah chapter sixty-four, verse six!"

"I agree with you, Mary," I said, causing her to take a step back and blink in shock.

"What? You do?" Now Mom raised an interested eyebrow at our discussion. And Lacey was on the edge of the couch, puzzled as well.

"Absolutely," I said, folding my hands in front of me.

"I don't get it," said Mary. "You're admitting defeat?"

"Oh, certainly not," I said, pretending to dust off the sleeves of my suit coat.

"So, what are you doing?" asked Lacey.

"I am relishing the setup Mary has given me."

"What setup?" asked Mary. I placed a hand on her shoulder—which she promptly brushed off—then straightened my tie, grinned, and took a deep breath.

"Allow me to enlighten you, little one. The fact is all our righteousness is filthy rags because Romans chapter three, verse twenty-three, says we have all sinned. Second, Romans chapter six, verse twenty-three, says that our righteousness is a gift from God, because Ephesians chapter two, verse eight, says we are saved by grace through faith not by anything we do lest someone should boast." I began to walk around the room like a teacher lecturing his class. "That word *faith*, Mary, is important because it is impossible to please God without it—Hebrews chapter eleven, verse one—and even though you can't see what's inside my head, God has promised that if anyone lacks wisdom, all he has to do is ask God for it—James chapter one, verse five—and God will give it liberally.

"So the way I see it, Pigtails Pappenfuss, in spite of the tendencies of your carnal nature described in First Corinthians chapter three, verse three, you are required to walk by faith and not by sight as Second Corinthians chapter five, verse seven, points out. So why don't you go upstairs and get into your closet as Matthew chapter six, verse six, directs, and pray for me as Jesus instructed in Matthew chapter five, verse forty-four, and let us all see you are a Christian by your love—John chapter thirteen, verse thirty-five. Somebody say Amen!"

Mary stood there, face bright red and fuming, but try as she might, she had nothing to say.

"Peter!" said Dad, amazed. "You just preached your first sermon—and it was good!"

"It would have been better," said Mom, bringing him back to the reality of his defeated daughter, "if it hadn't been directed at his sister." She steered Mary away from me and suggested they go get ready to leave. Mary complied with clenched fists. As she and Mom disappeared upstairs, Lacey got off the couch and shook my hand wide-eyed.

"I'm impressed, Peter. Your mind is almost as sharp as the clothes I picked out for you."

Dad clapped me on the shoulder. "That was really something, Son," he exclaimed. I exhaled and massaged my temples. "What's wrong?" he asked.

I shook my head. "I'm just glad it's over."

"How come?" asked Lacey. "Do you feel bad for your sister?"

"Oh, no," I said, making my way to the couch and fumbling for my iPod. "She had it coming. I'm glad it ended, because I don't remember any more Bible texts. Now, if you'll excuse me, I need to try and cram at least five more in there before the contest."

CHAPTER TWENTY-ONE

REGISTRATION AND AGGRAVATION

After a light lunch at Subway, we all headed over to the Radisson Hotel to meet Ms. Witherspoon and begin my afternoon of agony. I had felt fine before lunch—even after almost running out of texts when dueling with Mary—but as we arrived for lunch, the reality of the contest hit me. Mom *made* me eat a six-inch veggie sub because it would give me energy and not be too heavy—in case I thought the answer to the first question was to throw up on everybody. As we pulled into the parking lot, that scenario seemed likely.

"Can we go home, instead?" I offered.

"Are you feeling sick?" asked Mom, turning around to look at me.

"I think the real question is, Are you going to *be* sick?" said Mary with a smirk.

I glared at her. "Only if I keep looking at you."

"You'll be fine, Peter." Dad assured me. "Once we are registered and sitting down, you'll be fine. Most of those nerves come from not knowing what to expect. You'll see it's not so bad once we're inside."

I've never thought of my dad as a liar, but as we entered the enormous ballroom of the Radisson, I began to wonder. The ceiling was taller then our gymnasium, and the walls were full of mirrors and glittering lights, which made the five billion people packed in there seem like ten billion. To make matters worse, they were ten billion Snotgrasses—all kinds of kids with bow ties, glasses, and smug looks were waltzing around with their proud parents. The placed reeked of dork. I was the odd man out—and everyone sensed it.

"Quite a crowd, huh, Peter?" said Ms. Witherspoon who met us with a smile just inside the door.

"Don't remind me," I said, feeling even more ill.

"You'll be OK," she said, putting a hand on my shoulder before greeting my folks. "How are the proud parents doing?"

"A little nervous," admitted Mom with a laugh, "but not as bad as Peter." Ms. Witherspoon nodded and then looked at Mary.

"And how are you, Mary? What do you think of all this?"

"I'm still amazed he got this far," said Mary absentmindedly, without looking at the teacher. Ms. Witherspoon laughed.

"Well," said Dad stretching, "might as well get Pete all signed in. It'll take at least ten minutes to wade through this throng of people."

"Thanks, Dad," I said.

"For what?"

"For pointing out all the people—it calms me."

"Sorry, sport."

I got several stares as we made our way to the registration table. It was located just a few feet ahead of the entrance to the ballroom in front of several cubicle structures. Two men and one woman were operating the desk. The two men looked stiff, like corpses, with pale skin and dark suits. The lady sat between them. She was rather large and had bright red hair that stood at least two feet tall on top of her head. Of course, we went to her.

"Good afternoon," she said. She had more makeup on her face than my mom uses in a year.

"Hello," I answered with my hands in my pockets. "Some gathering, huh? I bet every nerd in the state is here."

She stared at me and pursed her lips. "Only the ones from the city, young man. And *don't* make fun of nerds," she said in a deep voice, standing up to glower down at me. "They will be the ones with all the money when you are older. Now then," she continued in a nicer tone as she sat back down, "what is the name of this angelic creature?" She was looking at Mary.

"Mary Pappenfuss," said my sister with a toothy grin.

The red-haired lady nodded. "Lovely. Let me just check to find your name . . ." She pulled a pencil from her hair and began scanning a piece of paper on the desk when my dad interrupted.

"Oh, I'm sorry. Mary is only in the third grade. It's my son, Peter, who is competing."

She raised an eyebrow. "You mean this one, here?" she said, pointing at me with a pencil. I bet she had fifty of them stuck in that hairdo of hers.

"That's correct," said Dad politely. She exhaled and shook her head. She looked surprised when she found my name.

"Peter Paul Pappenfuss, eh?" I nodded. "Very well," she said, marking off my name visibly annoyed. Then she reached under the table and pulled out a name tag and a manila envelope. "This is a preliminary test that all competitors must take before the actual contest begins."

"What!" I said shocked.

"Don't interrupt, young man, for I will not repeat myself." I bit my tongue and nodded for her to continue.

"Each competitor will go to one of the test-taking booths behind this desk, and an attendant will give you thirty minutes to take the preliminary test. Don't dawdle. If you fail to complete all the questions, the empty spaces will count against you." I swallowed hard, glad I had eaten only a six-inch sub—otherwise, I would have lost it right then and there.

"After the time is up and you hand in your test, you will be free to wander the building for . . . ," she checked her watch, "another hour before the top twenty-seven scores are announced."

I felt my stomach bubble with anxiety. "What happens if you aren't in the top twenty-seven," I asked.

Her mouth twitched into a half smile, and her dark eyes sparkled. "*Then* you don't move on to the main competition."

I honestly don't know why some people are selected to work with children when their personalities clearly suggest they should be working with cardboard boxes or ill-tempered sea creatures. This woman was out to get me. Suddenly, I felt my mom's hand on my shoulder and heard her whisper in my ear. "Don't worry about her, Peter; she isn't in charge of how well you do."

"I'm sorry," said the woman. "What was that, Mrs. Pappenfuss?"

"Oh nothing," Mom replied. "I was just reminding Peter to do his best." The woman snorted and shook her head. My parents were not impressed.

"Well, if we have only an hour, we had better get started," Dad said coolly.

The woman held out the envelope, but when I tried to take it, she held on tightly and stared intensely at me. "I must also remind you that any lack of sportsmanship or hooliganism will not be tolerated. And do not open the envelope until you're told. Is that clear?"

"As clear as your love of children, ma'am," I said, smiling. Her face turned red with embarrassment, but she did release the envelope.

* * * *

It took a few minutes to get to the testing cubicles. When one became available, I was handed over to a man a little older than my dad, while my parents and Mary were directed to a waiting area.

"So, what's your name?" asked the man. He was wearing a sharp charcoal suit, a bright green tie with pinstripes, and his flawless dark hair had flecks of silvery gray in it.

"Peter Pappenfuss."

He smiled and shook my hand as we made our way to my booth—which was the last one on the end. "Nice to meet you. I'm Steven Larson." He had a good grip, unlike some of the older ladies in the church that make you feel like you are holding a dead fish. "What school are you from?"

"Davenport Junior Christian Academy."

He smiled warmly. "Oh, yes. I'm familiar with that school. You had a bit of an exciting church service a while back, if I'm not mistaken."

I groaned.

"Oh! Sorry. I didn't mean to bring up a sore subject."

I shrugged. "It's OK, I guess. It's just that there are a lot of hopeful people expecting me to do well here so I can help earn money to repair the damage that took place during that exciting church service."

Mr. Larson got a serious, but sincere, look on his face. "There's a lot of pressure on you, isn't there?" he asked.

Normally I wouldn't be so talkative to someone I had just met, but this man was easy to talk to, and it felt good to get it out. "Yeah, but my dad, who's the pastor, said it doesn't matter what happens—God will provide. The church, for the most part, feels the same way and are behind me no matter what."

He smiled. "Your dad sounds like a good man, and it sounds like you have a good church family."

"Yeah, they're alright."

"So, are you OK?"

"Well, I feel a little sick because of nerves. And that redheaded ray of sunshine at the registration desk didn't do anything to help."

Mr. Larson laughed out loud, a rich and genuine laugh, and patted me on the back. "Oh, yes," he said, wiping his eyes, "Mrs. Grossbauer."

"*Mrs.* Grossbauer?" I asked with a smile. Steven nodded. "She's married?"

"To a man who deserves to be on every prayer list in Davenport," he replied.

We both laughed, and I began to feel at ease. Mr. Larson showed me to my cubicle, which had a blue curtain covering the entrance so I wouldn't be distracted by anything outside. It also had little writing shelf built into it and a comfortable-looking chair. A clock hung right above the writing area.

"Well here it is, Peter." I took a deep breath and was going to sit down when he stopped me. "Hey, Peter, let me pray with you first. It's just something I do for everyone, but I really like you. You're quick-witted. Let me have a special prayer for you, then I'll let you know when to begin—OK?"

I was grateful for his support, and his prayer really helped me relax. His words were carefully chosen, and he made the prayer personal to my situation. Then he pulled out my chair and told me I could open the envelope.

"OK, Peter—it's one-thirty. There are thirty questions—so a minute for each. I will come back at two o'clock and get you."

"Thanks, Mr. Larson."

"Call me Steven."

Then he closed the curtain, and I began the test.

CHAPTER TWENTY-TWO
WAITING FOR JUDGMENT

"Has it been an hour yet?" I asked.

"Peter, you asked me that question five minutes ago," said Mom, "and I told you that it had been fifty minutes. Now it has been fifty-five minutes. You can see the clock as clearly as I can. In five more minutes, it will be an hour."

The last fifty-five minutes had been extremely tense. I had completed all but one question on the preliminary test when Steven told me my time was up. I felt so stupid telling him that I hadn't answered all the questions. He said it was in God's hands and not to worry about it. Dad, Mom, and Ms. Witherspoon said the same thing when I found them in the waiting area and told them how it went. But I could tell they were nervous.

Other families and teachers looked nervous as well—except for a few. One kid in a sweater vest, khakis, and a red bow tie emerged from the testing area almost skipping and told his parents, "I *know* I got them all right; it wasn't that hard." I tried to think of a way to lock him in a closet, so he wouldn't be there when his name was announced.

"So," said Mary who was sitting on the other side of Dad, clearly out of my reach, "*one* little question." I could feel my blood boil. "What was it?"

"It was on probability," I said, gritting my teeth.

"The probability of what?"

"The probability of little sisters surviving until their next birthday when they repeatedly make their older brothers angry."

"Peter!" scolded Mom.

"She's trying to push my buttons, and you know it," I responded.

"I still don't like threats, Peter."

"I know, I know—hey, Dad," I said, "can I see your cell phone? I'm going to call Harley to take my mind off of these last few minutes." Dad handed me his black phone, and I dropped it on the floor by accident.

"Hey, be careful, Peter," said Dad.

"Looks like Captain Sweaty Palms has returned," said Mary. I didn't respond but dialed Harley's number. I still couldn't believe his parents let him have a cell phone—and mine didn't.

"Hello? Peter?"

"Yeah, it's me."

"What's going on?"

"I'm sitting in a waiting room with forty Snotgrass clones."

"Gross. Bet you wish you had a dodgeball."

"Well, that would take care of the competition, but not my sister teasing me about not answering one question on the qualifying test."

"You had to take a test?"

"Yeah, we all did. The top twenty-seven scores compete. The rest go home."

"That's awful—and you say you missed a question?"

"Well, I may have missed more . . . ," at this everyone looked at me, and I scowled and stood up to walk to a corner of the room with a little more privacy, "but I know I missed one for sure because I left it unanswered. They gave us only thirty minutes."

"Dirty," said Harley.

"You're telling me," I continued. "And to make matters worse, a lot of these kids came out of the testing area practically skipping because they did so well."

"Did anybody else miss one?"

"Oh, yeah," I said. "I've seen at least five kids come out crying—one was a boy."

"Poor sap—buckled under the pressure."

"Yep."

"So, when do you find out if you made it?"

"Who knows? Supposedly in a few minutes. The last kid ended his test twenty minutes ago, and we've all been in this side room attached to the ballroom ever since."

"Yikes. So how are you feeling?"

"You know when you fell for Ms. Cracklestaff's evil plan in Sabbath School and ate all that candy?"

"That bad, huh?"

"Worse."

"Well, at least you haven't cried like the one kid."

"True. Anyway I . . . *wait*! Someone official is coming into the room! Oh no! He's being followed by the redhead and her army of the undead—"

"WHAT?"

"Hang on, Harley . . . they are about to announce the names!"

"Undead? Redhead? At the Radisson?"

"*Sssshhhhh!* OK? They're thanking us all for participating . . . blah, blah, blah, . . . 'you're all winners' . . . OK, here are the names . . ."

I watched the official, flanked by the redhead and her two minions, stand in front of the room and read the names from a podium with a microphone. Harley was yelling at me on the phone about me not giving him the play-by-play, but I was too mesmerized to respond.

"Number one: Ted Smith," announced the official. There was some clapping, and the kid with the sweater vest beamed as his parents hugged him. "Number two: Denise Livingstone." Again more clapping as a brown-haired girl with large green glasses stood and took a bow. "Number three . . . , number four . . ."

"PETER!" yelled Harley on the cell phone so loud I could hear him without having to hold it up to my ear. "WHAT NUMBER ARE THEY ON? ARE YOU IN?"

"Keep it down!" I hissed. "It's going to be hard enough getting in without you screaming on the phone and embarrassing me. They're on number sixteen . . . seventeen . . . eighteen." My name still hadn't appeared among the chosen few who were basking in the love and support of their families and teachers.

I could see my parents and Ms. Witherspoon frantically looking for me, but I ducked behind a few celebrating people who were on their feet. I was close to the exit as well. If I lost, I didn't want to look at their faces. I would rather take a walk in the parking lot by myself.

"Peter! What number? Come on, man!"

"Number twenty-two: Mia Wong. Number twenty-three: Mervin Samples. I dunno, man. I don't think I made it." I could feel a lump in my throat and heaviness in my chest at the thought of all my hard work being for nothing. I wouldn't even get to compete. I did all that work just to fail another test.

"Peter!" cried Harley. "Hang in there! Keep the names coming! This is worse than the time I watched you beat the last boss on Mario Galaxy! Peter?"

"Number twenty-five: Alberto Ramirez . . . number twenty-six: Kelsey Williams. Just one more left. And number twenty-seven . . ."

"Peter? Peter! Are you there? I heard a noise, and now I'm hearing applause. PETER, YOU NINCOMPOOP, ANSWER YOUR STUPID PHONE!"

"Harley! Shut up!" I snapped.

"For crying out loud, Peter, didn't you hear me?"

"Oh, I heard you alright—along with everybody else in the room, you numskull."

"What do you mean? What happened?"

"Well, my hands have been sweaty, and when they announced my name as number twenty-seven, I got so excited that the phone slipped out of my hand, and when I went to pick it up, I accidentally kicked it into the center of the room—right by the podium—with the speaker on. *Everybody* heard you call me a nincompoop. Including . . ."

"Wait, wait! Did you say that you were number twenty-seven? Is that what all the noise is in the background?"

"Yeah," I said, grinning from ear to ear as Mom, Dad, and Ms. Witherspoon hugged me. "I'm in!"

CHAPTER TWENTY-THREE
ROUND ONE

The first round of the competition was to begin exactly one hour from the time they announced the twenty-seven competitors. At that time, they would open the ballroom for general admission, and classmates, friends, and extended family would be allowed in. As for those of us who were actually competing, we would have to meet in the side room for prayer and instruction fifteen minutes before the contest and then take our seats, which would be in front of the stage area.

The contest was fairly simple in the way it was organized. The twenty-seven of us would be divided into groups of three. Each of these nine groups would compete for ten minutes, with the winner of each group moving on to the next round. The next round would involve three groups of three, who would compete for fifteen minutes, with the winners moving on to the final round, which would begin at 7:30 P.M. That is, unless some kid had a heart attack from stress—which was likely, based on what I had seen since they announced the competitors.

Soon after we celebrated my narrow victory as number twenty-seven, parents and forlorn children who hadn't been successful were asked to leave. Not since I volunteered in Cradle Roll had I seen so many temper tantrums. One kid refused to go and lay down on the floor. His embarrassed mother—an ample woman with arms the size of tree trunks—merely grabbed him by his kicking feet and dragged him out the door.

Another girl was so upset that she just stood in the middle of the room and screamed with rage—between sobs.

"Do you think she needs medication?" I asked Ms. Witherspoon, who was watching the girl's parents frantically doing everything they could to calm her down. She shook her head.

"No, Peter," she sighed, "she probably needs parents who don't put so much pressure on her—a lot of these kids do. You're very lucky, Peter." She was right. For as soon as she said that, I saw one dad marching his family out the door, with a face even more red than Principal Purvis's when he's angry.

"If you had just studied a little harder!" he scolded his son who was visibly upset with himself—not to mention his life in general.

Dad and Mom had been talking with the officials to get exact times for when we needed to be at the first round, but they walked over to us shortly after the march of shame made its way to the parking lot.

"Peter," said Mom, "I know we have told you this—and we are very proud of you for making it this far—but really, it's OK if you don't win."

Dad nodded. "That's right, Peter. We are more than impressed with you making it this far." Mary just stood there.

"And what about you?" I asked her.

She shrugged. "I'm not making a comment one way or the other," she said, primping with her baby blue dress and not making eye contact.

"My prayers are answered, then," I shot back. This time she did make eye contact, and it wasn't a happy look. But before she could reply, Dad ushered us to some seats away from all the people leaving the Radisson.

"Alright, before we go celebrate Peter's first victory of the day, there are a few rules. As you know from the announcement, we need to be back here fifteen minutes early, which gives us about forty minutes. When we return, Peter will have one form to fill out, so they can announce his name and school properly when it's his turn to compete."

I felt my stomach squirm when he said the word *compete*. I wonder if this is how skydivers feel when they are about to jump out of a plane.

"Now, then," Dad continued, "because they are expecting a lot of people, space is limited—and you are allowed to invite only fifteen people besides immediate family and your teacher."

"Sounds like plenty to me," I said.

"Really?" asked Mom.

"Sure. The less people watching me, the less nervous I'll be."

"That's one way to look at it, I guess," replied Mom. "So, who will you invite besides your class?"

"I have to invite my entire class? How about just a few of them?"

"Peter," said Ms. Witherspoon, "they have been a part of this alongside you, and it wouldn't be fair if you didn't at least invite them."

"Fine," I said. "I guess that leaves only two slots."

"Um . . . , just one, actually," said Dad.

"Dad, don't tell me that you need me to tutor you in basic math—even Mary knows fifteen minus thirteen is two."

Dad gave me a half smile. "No, Peter, I can do math . . . It's just that I have invited someone already."

"The head elder?" I asked.

"Er . . . no, Peter . . ."

"The hippie who came and sang to our class, . . . what was his name? Rainbow or Echo or something?"

"Ah, . . . no, Peter."

"I know, the little old lady who gave me the Daniel scripture."

Dad shook his head.

"Then who else is there? Everybody else who has been involved in this process has been . . . wait! No . . . Dad, you didn't!"

He nodded. "Principal Purvis has a right to be here as principal of your school, and he was the one who assigned you the tutor. He was the one who allowed you to compete, and he was the one who—"

"Has made my life miserable for the past three months! Did you forget his outburst on Friday?"

"Peter, that isn't kind. And, no, I haven't forgotten. But I think he deserves a chance to be here. And on Sabbath, he specifically asked me to let him know if there was a way he could come."

"Oh, good! Then he has something extra special planned for me. I wonder if he is going to throw tomatoes at me or boo and hiss when I get an answer right or maybe he conned Mom into giving him some incriminating baby photos that he plans to flash on the big screen right in the middle of a hard question."

"Peter, this isn't up for discussion, and you would do better not to worry about him but focus on the task at hand."

"Besides," said Ms. Witherspoon, "if anyone does something to distract the contestants, I am sure they will be asked to leave. I saw several security guards in the area where they are setting up the stage."

"So, who do you want to invite, Peter?" asked Mom. "We need to know so we can call them and they can get here on time."

"I dunno," I said, crossing my arms. "Let Harley pick."

* * * *

"Man, there are a lot of people here!" said Harley as soon as he walked through the main entrance of the ballroom to meet us. He was right. The place was packed. "How many do you think there are?"

"Dad said capacity was around six hundred, so I guess that's about how many there are."

"I heard your parents invited Mr. Purvis."

"Yeah, you'll have to keep an eye on him in case he tries something."

"No worries. I'll sit right behind him, if I can, and thwart any plan he comes up with."

I smiled and clapped him on the shoulder. "Thanks, man."

"My pleasure. So, speaking of seats, where are we sitting? Did you get us the VIP section? Or the nosebleed?"

"I knew you'd ask, so while we went to Dairy Queen, I made Dad wait here until they had finished setting up. He scored us front row seats!"

"Sweet."

"I know, but hey, I've got to get in the prep room to get ready, so you should find your seat. My parents, Ms. Witherspoon, and almost everybody else is already there—except Mr. Purvis and whoever you invited. Say, who did you invite?"

Harley grinned. "You'll have to wait and see. She said she would be a little late."

* * * *

The atmosphere in the prep room was tense. I couldn't stop bouncing my legs as I sat, and several other kids were nervously going through flashcards and notes. One boy went through about six packs of orange Tic Tacs. I was sitting along the wall with the other twenty-six competitors. On my right was a pretty Asian girl, who looked totally composed, and on the left was a chubby young man who kept breathing into a paper bag.

"Are you alright?" I asked him.

He didn't even look up at me. "Don't . . . talk to me . . . I'll puke."

I turned to the girl on my right. She had her hair in a jet-black ponytail with a red ribbon and was looking straight ahead without blinking. "Pretty crazy, huh?" I said with a smile, looking for someone to commiserate with.

"Who? Me?" she snapped, twisting in my direction. Her eyes flashed with anger.

"N-no, I mean the contest."

"Oh, so the contest is for crazy people—is that it?"

My mind went blank, and I scrambled to find words to calm her down. "Th-that's not what I meant . . . I mean . . . uh . . . the environment is crazy . . ."

"So, this is the sort of place that makes people crazy, is that what you're saying?"

"Um . . . I guess so."

"So, are we all crazy, then? Or is it just you? Because I'm not crazy. I'm just fine. I'm going to win." I didn't know what to say, and she began to trail off, mumbling to herself, "I'm not crazy. I'm just fine. I'm going to win." I put my head in my hands and prayed that this would all be over soon. A few moments later, the door to the prep room opened, and the officials walked in—including Steven Larson.

"Good afternoon, boys and girls," he said, flashing us a warm smile. It had an effect on the whole room and even made the sick kid next to me put down his bag. "I'm sorry I'm a little late. We had a young man from one of the schools go missing. He went looking for a vending machine and ended up in the women's bathroom by mistake. Thanks to several screaming females, we were able to locate him."

Several people laughed. *Tommy Sneldon,* I thought, shaking my head.

"I know you must all feel nervous, but don't be. You are all here because you have worked hard and God has been watching over you. In about five minutes, we will all filter out to the very front row of seats, and we will call you up by threes. As you know, we will have ten minutes of questions. How many of you have seen *Jeopardy?*"

Everyone raised their hands.

"Excellent," he said, continuing. "Then you already know how this will work. When it's your turn, or when you have answered a question correctly, then you will pick a question from one of the categories. Each question is worth a different point amount based on its difficulty, with two hundred being the easiest and one thousand being the most difficult. When the question is read, the first person to buzz in with the correct answer will get the points. Don't worry about phrasing the answer in the form of a question. Is everything clear?"

We all nodded.

"Good! Then let's have prayer and go on out there."

CHAPTER TWENTY-FOUR
GAME ON!

When we emerged from the back room, the whole ballroom had changed. The main lights had been turned off, and illuminating the back wall, surrounded by chairs, was a huge glowing blue screen with the words: "Davenport Fifth Grade Christian Academic Jeopardy." Stage lights of various hues and colors also shone brightly on the stage area where the emcee's podium and contestants' booths were. The theme music from *Jeopardy* was playing, and people were clapping along—and some obnoxious older kids had gotten together in the back of the room and were humming the theme song.

"Ladies and gentlemen!" said a voice from out of nowhere. "Please welcome your area fifth-grade contestants!" The thundering applause rattled my nerves. It reminded me of the roar of the crowd at a Twins game I went to last summer. Except this time, I wasn't in the stands—I was the entertainment! I felt a lump in my throat and swallowed hard.

We contestants all filtered in and took our seats. The stage area was so bright that it was hard to make out the faces of people in the audience—a good thing if you ask me. Not that I would have looked anyway. I took my seat along with the others, and then I began counting by threes. I wanted to see who I would be competing against. It turned out to be "Bag Boy" and "I'm Not Crazy Girl." Great!

"Allllrighhhtt! Now, ladies and gentlemen, please welcome your host for the evening—and president of the local Christian Businessmen's Association—

Steeeeeeeven Larrrssoooon!" Another thunderous applause as Steven took the podium and began his welcome. I smiled. At least the host would be friendly and not someone like the red-haired fiend who was sitting offstage right in the "judges' corner" in case there was some uncertainty about the accuracy of someone's answer.

After a general prayer, the contest began. It went fast. The contestants were brilliant—acing subjects such as grammar, Bible, and history with ease. The first four groups of three flew by. Several kids nearly lost it when they were eliminated. However, Steven was smooth and reminded each of them that just for making it to the first round, they would be receiving a three-hundred-dollar gift card to Barnes & Noble to further their studies. This cheered up most of them, although a couple of basket cases exploded in the wings after they left the stage.

"OK, now I'd like to invite group number five—group number five—up to the stage." I took me thirty seconds and a nudge from "Bag Boy" to realize that I was in group five. I held my breath as I slowly stood up and walked numbly behind "I'm Not Crazy Girl," who was still mumbling to herself. Mr. Larson announced our names as we moved into the bright lights of the stage.

"First, we have Mia Wong from First Baptist Christian Elementary!" There was a good amount of applause, and "I'm Not Crazy Girl" took her place in the first booth, which would be on the left, if you were facing the stage. "Second, we have Peter Paul Pappenfuss from Davenport Junior Christian Academy!" I heard my parents cheer for me and Harley's voice above everyone's yelling, "Work it, Pappenfuss!" I felt cold and hot at the same time, as I squinted into the bright lights. As I walked past Steven, I looked at him, and he gave me a wink and a nod. It gave me enough strength to get to the middle booth and brace myself as Steven announced "Bag Boy," the third contestant in our group. Of course, he didn't call him "Bag Boy." "The third contestant in this group," Steven called out, "is Milford Carmichael from Holy Trinity Lutheran Elementary!" Even though he got tremendous applause, Milford still had his bag with him. I couldn't tell if the green hue on his face was from one of the colored stage lights or from his nausea.

Once "Bag Boy" was in place, Steven read the five categories of questions: science, math, English, geography, and pop culture. "We will begin with science. I will read the first question, and the first person to buzz in and answer correctly will have control of the board. Ready?"

Mia and I nodded, and Milford took a deep breath into his bag.

"What is the freezing point of water?"

I know that one! It's . . .

BUZZ!

"Yes, Milford?"

"Thirty-two degrees Fahrenheit."

"Correct! Milford, you have the board." I was stunned. It had all happened so fast—and from a guy who had his face in a bag, no less. Milford got two more correct answers from science before Mia headed him off and picked a question from geography.

I woke up from my daze to hear Steven saying, "Correct, Mia—the answer *is* Atlanta, Georgia. This brings your score to one thousand points. Milford has twelve hundred, and Peter has yet to score."

I was bombing—in the first round! And I had known the answer to half the questions; I just couldn't press the buzzer fast enough. Before I could wallow in total misery, a chant began to go up from the crowd. "Papp-en-fuss! Papp-en-fuss! Papp-en-fuss!" It was loud—loud enough to be more than just my fifteen guests.

"Whoa, folks!" said Steven, raising his hand to quiet things down. "It appears that Peter has a fan club rooting for him to get on the board. However, I must ask you to hold your encouragement until after a question is answered."

I found myself smiling, as I realized that it was cheering from those contestants who had been eliminated in the first round. I was the underdog—they could see it. Their cheering made me feel good, anyway, and I thought of all I had had to endure to get to this point—all everyone had had to endure, including persecution from jealous classmates. I closed my eyes for a moment.

Dear Lord, just let me get on the board. I don't need to win—just to represent my school, family, and friends well . . . and all those who didn't make it this far. I opened my eyes just as the next question was read.

"What is the capital of Canada?"

BUZZ!

"Ottawa!" I shouted into the microphone, causing everyone to jump.

"Wow! Those cheers certainly gave Peter an adrenaline rush—and he's right for six hundred points!" There was raucous applause now that all three of us were on the board and I was in the game at last.

"Your pick, Peter. What category would you like?" That was easy. Based on the typical kid in this contest and what the picks had been up until this point, I had one ray of hope.

"Pop culture."

"Pop culture it is. For two hundred points, what is the name of the Teenage Mutant Ninja Turtle with the red bandana?"

BUZZ!

"Raphael!"

"Peter scores another two hundred, bringing him to eight hundred points!" The crowd went wild. I was in my element.

"Pop culture for four hundred," I said with a grin.

Steven nodded. "For four hundred—and to tie the lead: the Nintendo Wii comes prepackaged with a sports game. Name the sports featured in this game."

BUZZ!

"Tennis, bowling, baseball, golf, and boxing!"

"Peter Pappenfuss gets the four hundred points and is now tied for first!"

I could hear my parents yelling in excitement and Ms. Witherspoon shouting, "Stay with what you know!" I did and aced the six-hundred-point question, bringing my total to eighteen hundred. Mia was still fuming with only a thousand points, and Milford was at twelve hundred.

"OK. Well done, Peter. It is now the one-minute warning, so pick fast, and all of you buzz in as quickly as you can. Remember, you don't have to pick low numbers. You can go straight to the thousand-point questions. Peter, it's your . . . what is that sound? Is someone wheezing?" It took ten seconds of our precious time to realize that Milford was breathing into his bag near the microphone.

"Put the bag away, Milford!" called his mom from the audience. With a shaky hand, he put it down, looking even greener than before.

"OK, Peter—hurry and pick."

"The usual."

"OK, pop culture for eight hundred. What doll brand comes out with a Christmas edition every year?"

BUZZ!

"That would be Barbie," said Mia with a maniacal laugh. She was right. Now, she and I were tied with thirty seconds left. Not that I would have answered that question even if I could. It would be humiliating—but now I was in trouble.

"Mia, you have control of the board."

"Geography for a thousand, please."

"In 2000, which state had a presidential voting mishap that required a recount?"

BUZZ!

"Florida!"

"Right! Mia is now the leader with twenty-eight hundred points. Peter is in second place with eighteen hundred, and Milford, with twelve hundred, had—better get that bag to his face because he is turning dark green! With twenty seconds to go, it's your pick, Mia!"

She looked at me. "Pop culture for a thousand!" It was a dare. She was basking in the glory of her own intellect and felt assured of her win. All at once the words, *BONUS QUESTION* flashed on the screen.

"Oh! This indicates that whoever answers this question correctly will be offered a bonus question! Now, for a thousand points, who is the leader of the Transformers?"

BUZZZZZZZZZZ!

"OK, we hear you, Peter!" said Steven, covering his ears and motioning for me to stop buzzing. "What's your answer?"

I released my grip on the buzzer and with my heart nearly beating out of my chest, answered, "Optimus Prime!"

"Correct!" I heard my classmates scream with glee amid the applause, and then everyone got silent—especially Mia who was now white with horror, realizing her gamble had not paid off. "Now for the win, Peter—the bonus question: can you spell *Optimus Prime*?"

My mouth went dry, and my memory flashed to the package my dad had given me a couple of months ago. It was still in my treasure chest—and still clear as a bell in my mind's eye.

"O-P-T-I-M-U-S P-R-I-M-E."

"We have a winner!" shouted Steven. People were on their feet clapping, and I felt a little queasy. But not as queasy as Milford, who lost it right then and there to commemorate my victory.

CHAPTER TWENTY-FIVE
SEMI-FINALS

Both Milford and Mia received a three-hundred-dollar gift card to Barnes & Noble, and I was told to go back to the side room where I could meet with my family and teacher once the other teams had finished. I felt light-headed leaving the stage. Not just because I couldn't believe my victory, but because I knew I had been lucky. That last question could have been on anything, and the next round would be harder—and so would the competitors.

The room had a few refreshments, and the winners of the earlier rounds were greedily taking advantage of them. I got a couple cookies and some punch and sat by myself—just wanting to collect my thoughts. Others were doing the same. These winners seemed much more together than the initial twenty-seven.

After about twenty minutes, I struck up a conversation with the boy who had won the first round. We met at the refreshment table loading up with another handful of cookies. He had dark skin, short curly black hair, and a Batman watch. His name was Gabriel.

"It was awful going first; I thought I would be sick," he volunteered.

"One of the kids in my round *was* sick," I told him, "all over the stage!" We both laughed, and I think we both felt better.

"Poor guy," said Gabriel, taking a sip of punch. "I don't know about all this."

"All this what?"

"The contest. I mean, it's cool that they want to encourage education and donate money and all—but it's making us all nuts."

"Are you saying I'm crazy?" I replied with a half grin, remembering my chat with Mia.

"Absolutely," he said with a smile of his own.

"Well, crazy or not, we had better load up with more cookies. We'll need the power of a sugar rush to survive this next round. I don't know about your mom, but if mine sees me eat more than two cookies, she flips out."

"Good point," Gabriel said—and we both loaded our plates full of cookies and sat down to discuss who was the best Batman villain. It was nice to find another normal person in this crowd of brains. Part of me hoped we wouldn't have to compete against each other. It wasn't long before our families started arriving and kids began cramming the remainder of their cookies in their mouths.

I parted company with Gabriel and was subsequently greeted by hugs and kisses from Mom, Dad, and Ms. Witherspoon—and a high five from Harley, who sneaked in with the family.

"That was a nice piece of work, Pete, lulling her in like that—then WHAM! Optimus Prime, baby!"

"Harley," said Mom, with a warning in her voice. He understood immediately.

"I mean, congratulations," he said soberly, extending a hand. "It's a shame all of you can't be winners." He looked at my mom, and she smiled her approval. But when she turned away, he winked at me.

"So, what's going on out there?" I asked him. "How is Mr. Purvis taking things?"

"Actually, Mr. Purvis isn't here. Maybe he chickened out. As far as the action goes, nothing happened after you left the stage that was as interesting as your round—no one got sick, and the last few rounds, certain kids just controlled the board. Especially two girls—Sally and Jill. They were amazing." My whole family agreed with Harley that these two girls were very talented.

"Are they in here?" I asked. Dad pointed them out. One had brown hair, and the other was a redhead—yet, somehow, they both reminded me of what Mary will be like in two or three years. Graceful, polite, and glowing in her own superiority. "Marvelous!" I grumbled.

"Nah, don't worry," said Harley, "they might get hung up on a category like the two contestants you beat."

"Not likely," I said. "That was a fluke."

"Now, Peter," said Dad, kneeling down to look me in the eye, "it could be more than that. God could really be looking out for you here. Don't take these little miracles too lightly."

"However," said Mom, folding her arms and tapping her foot, "you may want to take the refreshments more lightly." She wiped a hand across my mouth, and there was the chocolate-chip evidence all over her finger. "Honestly, Peter, how many cookies have you had?"

"Not as many as Gabriel."

"Who's Gabriel?" asked Ms. Witherspoon. I pointed him out across the room—he was praying with his family.

"He's probably the only other sane person in this place," I said. "Anyway, did they say what we are supposed to do next?"

"Yes. Actually, you don't have much time. They said it would only be a fifteen-minute break and then they would start the semi-final round—which leaves us about five minutes. We should probably have prayer, like your friend's family is doing, and then head back out there."

Mom and Dad and my other visitors left after prayer, and Mr. Larson came in to congratulate all of us and pray with us before beginning the competition again. For the semi-final round, the drill was the same. We would all go out and take our seats, then each group of three would be called up in turn, to compete. After Mr. Larson prayed, we all got in line and filed out into the ballroom again to more thunderous applause. This time, I was seated with the first group, and when they called us up, I really and truly did *not* feel ready. Maybe it was the cookies, but I felt heavier and slower. *Where was that sugar rush?*

The semi-final round proceeded much the same as the earlier rounds, with the categories being: biology, famous battles, long division, Christian music, and sports. Again, I was placed in the middle booth, but this time both of the other contestants were boys. I was glad Gabriel wasn't one of them. The boy on the right was Eduardo Gonzalez—a studious-looking guy dressed in khakis, a blue shirt, and thin, round glasses. The boy to my left was Mervin Samples. He wore his pants up past his neck like my grandpa does, so if there is a flood, the water won't come close to getting his trousers wet. His hair was parted in the middle, with both sides slicked down—and he had a pencil behind each ear. Normally a Grade A nerd such as this wouldn't faze me, because I could merely retreat to the sports category—but he was wearing sneakers with the logo of the Denver Broncos. Something told me this round was going to be hard.

My confidence was further shot when Steven told me I could pick first, since my score in the previous round was the lowest of the three contestants in this round. Naturally, I went with sports and was quickly on the board with two correct answers and six hundred points. However, the rest of the match was a dogfight. Eduardo tied me by answering the six-hundred-point sports question correctly. Then he devastated both Mervin and me by clearing out the entire Christian music category, bringing his total to thirty-six hundred points.

Mervin struck back and showed his prowess by stealing the first biology question, then quickly snapping up the two remaining sports questions, giving him two thousand points. I fought back by answering some famous battles questions and taking a risk by picking the thousand-point biology question—which, fortunately, happened to be on whales. Mervin made a mad dash through several long division questions before Eduardo stopped him. They were both incredibly fast with their buzzers, and it was all I could do to stay in the game. With only thirty seconds left in the round, the scores were

Mervin: 4,000

Alberto: 3,800

Me: 3,100

When Mervin selected the final question in the famous battles category, I resigned myself to defeat. However, as Steven read the question, something in the air began tickling my nose. I sneezed—which caused me to involuntarily push the buzzer at the exact moment Steven finished the question—a good half second before either Eduardo or Mervin! The question was about the Trojan war and the method used for getting inside the walls of the city.

"The men made a wooden horse, and when the enemies brought it inside the city, the soldiers leaped out. Is that right?"

Steven smiled. "Peter Paul Pappenfuss has done it again!" The crowd went nuts again, and this time, both contestants shook my hand as they were awarded their one-thousand-dollar runner-up prizes for the semi-final round.

CHAPTER TWENTY-SIX
TAKING A BREAK

The rest of the semi-final rounds went swiftly, and then there was an hour break for supper. Gabriel, unfortunately, didn't win—but he was close. He said he would have won, but the judges decided that his winning answer wasn't quite complete, so an opponent grabbed his answer and expanded on it. My head was swimming as my family and excited classmates met me in the lobby. Everybody said they were impressed and that it was the best show they had ever seen.

"You looked magnificent, Peter" said Lacey, fussing with my tie and grinning. "This is some of my best work."

"That sneeze was well placed, Peter. How did you do it?" asked Gretchen, as we made our way out of the Radisson.

"It wasn't planned, you dimwit," said the unmistakable voice of Lucas Snodgrass. He was walking just behind us. "It was dumb luck—emphasis on the *dumb*."

"Lucas, I think you need to go find your parents," said Mom. Lucas didn't say anything. He wasn't as bold alone as he was when his uncle was around. *I wonder where he is, anyway?*

"I didn't see your parents in there," I said to Lucas with fake concern—then snapped my fingers in false realization. "Oh, that's right—only family of the *contestants* get to come inside. Silly me!"

"Enjoy it, Peter Paul," he hissed. "Dumb luck won't help you win against Sally and Jill." I stopped smiling.

"Oh, you didn't know?" he laughed.

"That's enough," said Ms. Witherspoon. "Peter, leave Lucas alone and vice versa," she added, looking at Lucas. He continued laughing and made his way to find his parents.

"Don't give it another thought, Peter," she said, "everybody has seen you answer more than your share of questions. Now, let's get everybody together for supper. Taco Bell is just across the parking lot, and we had better hurry, or there won't be anything left. And Tommy—DON'T wander off!"

"But I don't *want* Taco Bell," whined Wesley.

"Then you can sit quietly and eat nothing," said Ms. Witherspoon. Wesley decided Taco Bell would be fine after all.

Supper came and went too quickly. A burrito should never be eaten with this much stress, and I hoped I wouldn't have to use the bathroom in the middle of the final round. Another hindrance to my dining pleasure was the barrage of questions and comments I kept getting. Melissa said she was proud of me for remembering one of the most famous horses in history and asked if I remembered any others. Jennifer quizzed me on football teams, Gretchen on mythology, and Sam tried to convince me that if I wanted to have a real sugar rush to enhance my performance, I should eat three Choco-Tacos like he was doing. Which was probably true—he was quivering like a lab rat and spilled his water on himself—twice.

The worst was when the conversation drifted to Sally and Jill and their previous performance. Sally had ended her round with forty-five hundred points, while the next runner-up had only fourteen hundred. Jill had forty-eight hundred points, with the second-place contestant having only eight hundred! Someone said their scores would have been even higher if the other contestants hadn't wasted time by pressing their buzzers in the desperate hope of answering a question—which they couldn't.

"There's no doubt about it, Peter," said Dad, finishing his drink, "the final round is going to be tough. We'll have special prayer for you. Just try to stay calm. Those other contestants who lost got nervous and made hasty decisions."

"Would it be a hasty decision to just take the runner-up prize and call it good?"

"YES!" said everyone in unison. I sighed and took another drink of soda before throwing my trash away. I couldn't shake what Lucas had said— *"Dumb luck."* I mean, what if he were right? I was an intellectual pygmy, compared to Sally and Jill. What if my luck ran out?

"OK, gang," said Dad, standing up, "we had better follow Peter's example and finish up. He needs to get back, so he can have time to clear his head."

As we made our way back through the parking lot, cars were returning from the brief supper break. I recognized some of the kids in them as runner-up contestants. I couldn't believe they were staying till the end. I wanted to leave so bad I could taste it. Well, it would all be over in about ninety minutes. The sky was dark now, and the air was chilly. At least it was warm inside. I didn't say anything as we walked, but listened to the laughter and predictions of my classmates.

"I say Peter gets eight thousand, Jill thirty-two hundred, and Sally two," laughed Harley.

"No, no," insisted Jennifer, "not even close. Peter will have thirty-four hundred, Jill thirty-two hundred, and Sally an even three thousand."

You're all too generous, I said to myself. Mom noticed my lack of enthusiasm and put her arm around me as we walked.

When we arrived at the lobby entrance, we were greeted by none other than Principal Purvis! He looked tired and a little worn. He was wearing a light-colored suit and a dark tie. He didn't appear angry—but I could tell he had been waiting for us.

"Uh, good evening," he said weakly. Everyone stopped and stared— unsure of what to do next or what was about to happen.

"Good evening," said Dad, coming from behind Mom and me. "I'm glad you could make it."

Principal Purvis looked at me. "I understand, Peter, that you are in the final round?"

I didn't know how to respond. Was he setting me up for a slam? Was this an attempt to sabotage my already-nervous mind? I decided a simple answer would be best. "Yes, sir."

Without saying anything, he reached into his coat pocket and pulled out a white envelope. Everyone's eyes were fixed on it. Mr. Purvis turned it over a few times in his hands and then handed it to me. "For you to read. For you *only*. I just ask that you look at it before you begin the final round."

I took the envelope gently and looked down at it. It was plain white, sealed, and had my initials on it. Then Mr. Purvis nodded slightly and made his way into the building.

"That was the weirdest thing I've ever seen," said Harley.

"It *is* a little odd," agreed Dad, "but we don't have time to consider the situation. We need to pray and give Peter some time to honor his principal's request."

* * * *

The prep room was quiet. I sat along one wall, and Sally and Jill sat along another. We didn't make eye contact—just let ourselves get lost in thought. Dad, Mom, and Ms. Witherspoon had special prayer with me before going to take their seats. As he left, Dad encouraged me to look in the envelope from Mr. Purvis. I wasn't so sure. It was fifteen minutes until the final round began, and all I could do was turn the envelope over in my hands much the same way Mr. Purvis had.

If this was a final discouragement of some kind, I didn't want to hear it. And I couldn't imagine it being anything else. Still, Mr. Purvis hadn't said anything negative when he gave it to me—and Dad seemed sure that I should look at it. I just didn't know what to do. I wished I could have someone else read it first and tell me whether it was something I should know. As I mulled over whether or not to open the envelope, I heard a commotion outside the door.

"Let me in, I tell you! It's critical for his performance!" It was Harley's voice.

"Now, Son," said the voice of an official, "you need to take your seat—the contestants need time to think and prepare."

"Trust me—if he finds out that you didn't let us in, he will bad-mouth this contest to everyone in the community—and he could too! His dad's a pastor! He'll preach a sermon on it!" I got up quickly and went to the door and opened it.

The official was restraining Harley as best he could—until Harley stomped on his foot.

"Ow!" yelped the official, hopping on one foot.

"Let that be a lesson to you!" exclaimed Harley. "When power goes to your head, the result is sore feet!" I motioned for Harley to hurry into the room and apologized to the official, assuring him it was OK.

"Thanks, Peter! We're coming."

"We?"

"Yeah. I told you she would be late. Just arrived in the nick of time too!" That's right—Harley's guest, the one we'd let him pick! I hadn't even noticed her standing behind him. Allison Marie Swenson looked as beautiful as ever as she followed Harley into the room. We quickly went to my wall while Sally and Jill stared at us, puzzled. My hands began to sweat again, and I was at a loss for words. Thankfully, Harley spoke for me.

"He's delighted you're here, Allison," Harley said. She smiled. She was wearing dark jeans and a black top. Her hair was freshly cut with layers and blonde highlights. "As you can tell by the dumb grin on his face, he has been rendered a complete imbecile in your presence." I could have punched him.

"The reason I invited you here," Harley went on, "is that Peter believes that the last kiss you gave him was lucky."

"Harley!" I snapped. Allison just laughed—a beautiful rich laugh that made my toes tingle. Harley stepped behind Allison, leaving no roadblock between her and me.

"The real tragedy in all this, Allison, is that after Peter left the imprint of your lips on his cheek for more than seven hours, his cruel mother, fearing that it was making him deranged, made him wash it off!" That was it! Harley was going to have a final round of his own to contend with after the contest. A final round with me in the parking lot!

"So, what are you asking me to do, Harley?" Allison smiled and looked at me.

"I'm asking if you could find it in your heart to give Peter another good luck charm."

"You mean a kiss?"

Suddenly my mouth went dry—because I swallowed my own spit. I started to cough, wheeze, and tear up as I tried frantically to regain my composure.

"Harley!" I managed to croak, trying to clear my throat, "I will kill you . . . so help me."

"Oh, don't do that, Peter," said Allison. Then she kissed me on the right check! Then—to both our surprise—she quickly kissed my left cheek as well! I went numb and then warm, then giddy. I giggled—like one of my sister's friends—and threw in some sort of whistling, squeaking noise I had never made before. Harley was all smiles, raising his eyebrows up and down like a fool.

"That's some powerful stuff, Allison," said Harley. "Don't give him any more—he might not be able to walk or remember his name, much less the answers to any questions." She gave Harley a half hug and wished me luck. Harley followed her out the door, but not before giving me the thumbs up sign. Sally and Jill watched them leave and then looked at me and laughed quietly to themselves. I didn't care. I had the best friends in the world—and *two* good-luck charms! At this point, *nothing* could make me feel bad. I looked down at the envelope from Mr. Purvis and decided to open it.

CHAPTER TWENTY-SEVEN

PRINCIPAL PURVIS'S LETTER

October 21

Dear Peter,

How are you? Nervous, I imagine. I don't blame you. You have worked very hard, and even though everyone will support you no matter what, the pressure is no doubt very real and heavy.

I'm writing you, first and foremost, to apologize. I haven't been a good principal, much less friend, these past few months. I am sorry, Peter. You deserve to be treated better.

Now, before you think I am giving you this letter so I can attach myself to your success, please let me explain my behavior and why I have acted the way I have. My nephew, Lucas, has been having a rather hard time at home. His parents have been going through a rough patch and have separated—although they appear in public together at places such as church.

As you can imagine, this has been hard on him. It has also been hard on me, since his parents have requested that he stay with me at my home until they decide what to do about their marriage. Lucas has been my responsibility since August.

When I learned about this academic contest, I had high hopes for Lucas. Winning a competition such as this would be just the sort of thing to boost his spirits. It would be a chance to have something positive in his life, a chance to be a hero in spite of his family struggles.

Well, when it was announced that you would be the one to represent the school, I just . . . well, . . . I was disappointed. Not in you, please understand, but rather in the fact that Lucas would miss a chance that otherwise he might have had, had he not been sick that day.

Naturally, he was disappointed as well, and with the stress we were already having at home, you—unfortunately—became a target for our disappointment. It is inappropriate for any student to act out verbally against another—but it is even more so when a principal takes sides, plays favorites, and well . . . you know—you were there.

All I want to say, Peter, is that none of my actions reflect how I really feel. I am proud of you and pray that God will calm your nerves and bless you as He sees fit, as you end what has been a grueling three months.

I also ask that you give Lucas some grace. He is hurting and jealous and takes it out on whomever is around—even me sometimes.

In closing, I want to let you know that I will be taking a leave of absence from school for a few weeks until we can get our family straightened out. Please pray for us. I would also ask that you keep the details of this letter between you, me, and your father, whose permission I asked before I wrote you.

All the best,
Principal Purvis

CHAPTER TWENTY-EIGHT
THE FINAL ROUND

"Walter? Walter!"

"Yes, dear?"

"What's wrong with Peter? Why is he grinning like an idiot and staggering around up there like . . . *like he's drunk!*"

"I don't know, dear. Maybe it has something to do with the lipstick on his cheek."

"What? Where—which one?"

"Both of them, actually."

"Harley! What did you do?"

"Take it easy, Mrs. P. It was just for good luck, and besides, Peter said I could invite anyone I wanted to."

"Ha! That a boy, Harley! Let's hope it works."

"Walter!"

"Oh, it's just a little encouragement. He won't be too disturbed when he grows up."

"But . . . all that lipstick! That girl!"

"I think he'll be fine, Mrs. P. If he isn't, then you can blame the kisses."

"Harley, I will blame *you!*"

"Why? *I* didn't kiss him!"

"*Sssh!* They're starting!"

I wasn't sure exactly what my parents were arguing about with Harley, but I could guess. I could feel the two kisses glowing in the stage lights. After a couple of moments, I could also make out Mr. Purvis in the audience. He was sitting behind our class—alone. I couldn't make out the expression on his face. It was a mix of emotions. His letter made me feel the same way—mixed up. I wasn't sure what to think after reading it. I felt bad for him—and even Lucas. I guess Dad was right—they had their own issues to deal with.

I couldn't think of anything to do as I found myself staring at him. So I decided to give him a nod and a smile. He actually smiled back, although it wasn't a very big smile. Then, to my surprise, he gave me a thumbs up sign like Harley had done. It's strange to have someone who has been your enemy for so long suddenly support you.

My trance was broken by Steven Larson, who leaped onto the stage and welcomed the crowd. He had them all applaud the previous contestants before drawing everyone's attention to us finalists.

"And now for the final three—the ones who have fought their way to the top in order to win TEN THOUSAND DOLLARS for their school!" More applause. "Let's talk to them. First up is Sally Mortonhouse from Sacred Heart Catholic Elementary!" She received a huge response from the crowd. Her red hair came down to her shoulders and she was wearing her school uniform, which consisted of a white blouse and green plaid skirt. She had freckles that covered her pointy nose.

"Sally has swiftly made her way to the top after some staggering displays of intelligence and study. Hello Sally, how are you?"

"Fine, thanks. And you?"

"I'm really enjoying myself tonight. Tell us, what would you do with the ten-thousand-dollar prize money should you win it?" Her answer came so swiftly, I wondered if she hadn't rehearsed it.

"I would invest half of it in new computers for our technology lab and use the other half for worthy student funds." People clapped, and Steven nodded his approval.

"Good luck to you, Sally. Next we have the legendary Peter Paul Pappenfuss from Davenport Junior Christian Academy, who has had two very dramatic victories this afternoon—and it looks like two very dramatic smooches on the cheeks to boot!" I felt my face go red and could hear my mom mumble something from the audience.

"You know, Peter and I were talking earlier today about his school, weren't we, Peter?"

I nodded, unsure of where he was going.

"Peter, you had something unique happen to your school. Tell us—what happened?"

"Um . . . it blew up." There was a collective gasp and a few laughs from the crowd. Both Sally and Jill looked at me, stunned. "I mean, the boiler blew up," I explained.

"Yes, and wouldn't you know it, folks—the cost of repairs is *exactly* ten thousand dollars." There was some clapping and a few people began chanting, "We love Peter Paul Pappenfuss." While people were clapping, Steven leaned over and whispered in my ear briefly, "I'm praying for you, Peter. God will bless."

Then he moved on to Jill Swintin from King of Kings Methodist Elementary. She was the same height and build as Sally—tall and lanky—and she wore silver rings on all her fingers. When Steven asked her what she planned to do with the prize money if she won, she said she would use it to remodel their cafeteria.

Next, Steven directed everyone's attention to the big blue screen, so we could see the categories. "For this final round, each of the five categories will be Bible-related; after all, this is a Christian gathering of Christian schools, and it's fitting that the last round be about spiritual things." There were a few "Amens" and one "Preach it, brother!" "The categories are Bible stories, memory verses, books of the Bible, Proverbs, and life of Christ. We will play until the board is empty. I'll pick the first question, and the first correct answer will control the board. Are you ready?"

The three of us nodded. "Contestants, shake hands." I turned to Sally first. She smiled pleasantly and extended her hand.

"God bless you, Peter."

"You, too." Wow! She was nice. Then I turned to Jill, who also smiled when she shook my hand.

"Good luck."

I wished her the same. Then both girls shook hands, and I could hear them both say, "May the best *girl* win." They laughed quietly. I knew then that they were out to get me. Steven led us in a quick prayer before reading the first question for the round I had been dreading for three months.

"Life of Christ for two hundred points: where was Jesus born?"

Sally answered "Bethlehem" before I could even think about pressing my buzzer. She continued with life of Christ until she had wiped out the category and was sitting pretty with three thousand to my and Jill's big fat zeroes. However, after cleaning up one category, Sally apparently decided to let Jill have a turn. Jill proceeded to snatch every single question from the Proverbs category.

"They're pummeling him!" exclaimed Harley—a little too loud. A few people laughed nervously.

"Thanks, Harley," I muttered annoyed and not realizing how close I was to the microphone. Everybody laughed and looked at Harley, but the exchange seemed to break the tension.

Sally and Jill spent the next few minutes playing "keep away," with one answering a question from the books of the Bible category only to let the other answer the next question. They both had over four thousand points by the time that category was completed. They had big smiles on their faces, and their stupid parents were already down in front flashing their cameras at them—taking pictures of me, with a big zero on my screen, between the two girls. When Steven wasn't looking, both girls even pointed to my zero for the camera. They were probably planning to upload this horrible event onto their MySpace sites so the whole world could enjoy my shame.

I looked out at the crowd and saw a very worried Ms. Witherspoon and my two fretful parents, who were doing their best to smile—and, no doubt, think of what encouraging things they could tell me after my loss. Harley gave me a clueless look and lifted his hands in an "I dunno" gesture. My classmates all had heir eyes shut and were obviously praying for a miracle. The only person among them, besides Snotgrass, that was enjoying the show was Mary.

Mary—my alien sister.

She sat with her fat little hand in a bag of popcorn she had gotten in the lobby. She was swinging her legs and smiling at me in delight. She reminded me so much of the two girls who were toying with me on either side. But then I remembered that Mary was the one I had defeated that morning by quoting Scripture. That was it! This contest was no different. These two young ladies on stage were just overgrown Marys—aliens sent to steal money from Christian education. No wonder they were so intelligent. I smiled and laughed quietly to myself.

Jill noticed and gave me a puzzled look. "Are you losing your mind or something?" she whispered.

I shook my head and smiled.

"Then are you just resolving to quit so your mind can be at peace?" she asked sweetly.

I smiled even bigger and shook my head again.

"Then what is it?" she said crossly.

I leaned closer to her. "Tell your people they can have my sister back anytime they want, but they can't have my school. Once this is over, you have five minutes before I reveal to everyone who you really are."

"What? What are you talking about?"

"OK, Jill. It's your turn," said Steven.

Just as I had hoped, the alien girl picked memory verses.

"For two hundred points, what text says, 'If we confess our . . .' "

BUZZ!

"Peter Pappenfuss!" the crowd applauded, and both Sally and Jill looked stunned.

"First John chapter one, verse nine."

"Correct!"

The place went nuts! I looked at Jill. "Time to make ready your ship, E.T."

She stared at me aghast and confused, while I selected the next question—and answered it. More applause! In record time, I had cleared the memory verse category. Meanwhile, the girls struggled to regain their focus, devastated by my discovery of their true identities.

"The scores are: Sally, four thousand six hundred points; Peter, three thousand; and Jill, four thousand four hundred. It's still anyone's game as we head to the last category: Bible stories. Peter, you are in control—go ahead and select." I took a deep breath and chose the two-hundred-dollar question.

"For two hundred points," said Steven, holding out the card in front of him and pausing for dramatic effect, "in what Bible story does a man get swallowed by a fish?"

I slammed down on my buzzer—but was just a fraction of a second too late!

"That would be Jonah when he was fleeing from the Lord's call to go to Nineveh," said Sally smugly, smiling at Jill and me. Only Jill smiled back.

Oh man! Now they are in control again. Come on, Peter, don't sweat it . . . just calm down . . . you can do this . . . you can beat the alien girls . . . you can . . .

BUZZ!

"What?" I exclaimed, and everyone in the room stared at me. "Uh . . . sorry," I muttered. I couldn't believe I had gotten so lost in thought that I didn't even hear the last question. Jill answered it for six hundred big ones.

"The scores now stand with Jill in the lead with five thousand points; Sally in second, with four thousand eight hundred; and Peter remaining in third place with three thousand. If Peter fails to answer any of the following questions, he will be eliminated." Steven said it gravely—but not in a scolding tone. He said it as a warning—to wake me up and make me pay attention.

"I'll take Bible stories for eight hundred, please," said Jill.

"For eight hundred points, what story features a prophet hiding in the woods from an evil queen?"

BUZZ!

"Elijah—right after he wasted the Baal prophets."

"Peter, with a save!"

Once again, the crowd erupted; over the noise, I could hear Harley's voice saying, "I can't take it anymore!" I could barely take it myself. I felt a rush of blood leave my head and braced myself against the side of the booth.

"Close one, Peter! Well done!" said Steven, flashing me a toothy smile. "You are in control of the board."

"Whew!" I exhaled into the mike. People laughed. Notably, Sally, Jill, and my sister weren't impressed. I knew they were connected—and I could tell they were scared. The humans were going to win.

"I'll . . . uh . . ."

"Take your time, Peter; it's alright."

I gathered myself and looked up at the big screen. "Let's knock out that four-hundred pointer."

"OK, listen up, gang. For four hundred points: in the story in which God calls Moses to lead the Israelites, in what does God appear to speak with Moses?"

BUZZ!

"A burning shrub."

"Oooh! I'm not sure about that answer. Judges? Can we accept burning *shrub?*"

There was a moment of deliberation in which all of our hearts stopped beating. All eyes watched the redhead and her two henchmen discuss my answer. Finally, they agreed that "burning shrub" was acceptable, and I changed my opinion of that kind, beautiful redheaded woman, who gave me my four hundred points and kept me in the game.

"Ladies and gentlemen, we are in a situation more exciting than any of us could have predicted. The only question left is worth one thousand points. The scores are as follows: five thousand points for Jill; four thousand eight hundred for Sally; and staying alive with two consecutive correct answers and four thousand two hundred points, is Peter Paul Pappenfuss!" Whoops and hollers filled the ballroom, and each of us onstage trembled. I began looking in vain for one of Milford's paper bags to breathe into.

Steven continued. "The person who answers this next question will be our winner of the ten-thousand-dollar grand prize. And folks, I think it would be a good idea to pause right here for another word of prayer to invite the Holy Spirit into our hearts, to calm the contestants and give them courage." People readily bowed their heads, and Steven offered one final prayer.

"Dear Lord, You know the nerves in this building, and You know how hard each of the students has worked. We have come to the end of this contest, and we just want to invite Your presence to be with us as we bring things to a close. Thank You for this opportunity. Thank You for watching over each of the contestants. Stay close to us now, I pray in Jesus' name. Amen."

"Amen," said the audience.

"Now it comes down to the final question. Are you ready contestants?" We nodded and held our buzzers close. "For one thousand points, the lead, the game, *and* the ten thousand dollars—what Bible story contains the quote, 'But if not, let it be known to you, O king, that we do not serve your gods, nor will we worship the gold image which you have set up'?"

I couldn't believe my ears. I couldn't believe God would let this be the last question. I couldn't believe . . .

BUZZ!

. . . That I had been too stunned to press the buzzer before Jill! She beamed as she looked at both Sally and me. I felt sick. It was over. And it had ended with my own "theme text"—the very text my dad had preached on yesterday!

"Jill, for the win!" exclaimed Steven, pointing at her. Everyone held their breath.

"That would be . . . um . . . wait, . . . ah . . . when Moses brought down the Ten Commandments from Mount Sinai?"

There was a collective groan from the crowd, and Jill knew right away that she had lost. She hung her head and held back tears. Shock went through the crowd. I felt a surge of excitement go through me as Mr. Larson spoke.

"No, I'm sorry, that is not correct! The other contestants have a chance to steal!"

I went for the buzzer—but it slipped! *Stupid sweaty palms! I'm going to have corrective surgery when this is over.* I finally got a hold of it and went to push the button as hard as I could, when . . .

BUZZ!

"Sally gets to the buzzer first for the steal—and the WIN!"

She smirked and cleared her throat. I put my buzzer down and resigned myself to the loss. I prayed for the right words to say when people would inevitably ask how I was doing—which wouldn't be good.

"I believe," said Sally confidently, "that the story is from the book of Daniel . . ."

Yep, that's it. It's all over.

"When Daniel interprets the king's dream."

There was a great gasp, as the audience's breath was stolen away. Steven abandoned his composure and was leaping and yelling at the top of his lungs with excitement. "I'M SORRY, NO! THAT IS NOT CORRECT! PETER, YOU HAVE A CHANCE TO STEAL AND WIN! WHAT IS YOUR ANSWER?"

I felt every light, every eye, and every brain cell in the room glued on me. My legs shook, and the blood rushed from my head. I felt dizzy. Scared. Excited. And nauseous. I stopped blinking. I stopped breathing. It took every ounce of strength I had to squeak weakly into the microphone, "Fiery furnace . . . Daniel chapter three, verse eighteen."

Then something strange happened.

I saw Mr. Larson jump into the air and holler something—but I couldn't hear him. I saw people rushing the stage in slow motion. I looked up and saw balloons slowly drifting down from the ceiling. The lights danced all around me. The ballroom was spinning. My body felt heavy and light at the same time—and there was a tingling sensation in my hands and feet. Then a sound like rushing air filled my ears; my body felt like it was floating down a gentle stream. I smiled lazily, and wondered if the Lord was giving me a vision like He had done for people in the Bible. It was kind of a neat feeling.

Then everything went black!

CHAPTER TWENTY-NINE
THE AWAKENING

"Come on, Allison—you can't abandon him in his time of need!" cried Harley. I didn't see him at first, because the stage lights were blinding me and I was covered in balloons.

"Harley?" I said, dazed.

"He's awake!" Harley shouted, and there was an enormous roar from the crowd. It dawned on me that I had fainted—in front of everyone. Mom and Dad, along with Ms. Witherspoon, Mr. Larson, and my entire class were soon by my side, hugging me, laughing, and helping me to my feet.

"How . . . how long was I out?"

"Roughly five seconds," said Gretchen, who was on my right-hand side.

"You know," said Harley with his hands on his hips amid the hysteria, "if you could have waited another thirty seconds or so, I could have gotten Allison to give you CPR—*mouth to mouth*." He raised his eyebrows up and down and grinned.

"Harley O'Brien, you are a pervert," said Mary, who was standing to one side.

"Hey, someone has to look out for your brother!" he exclaimed.

"Yes, Harley," said Mom, "and that someone is me. And although I don't think you are a pervert, I am going to call your mother when we get home, because you are getting close."

As I looked around, I noticed I was completely surrounded by people taking pictures and wanting to shake my hand. It was all surreal. I felt like the president or a rock star. I still felt a little weak from all the strange feelings colliding in my legs, stomach, and head. I asked for help getting up. A couple of strong arms from behind me pulled me up effortlessly. I turned around to thank the person they belonged to.

Standing there was Mr. Purvis—Principal Purvis—with a stoic smile!

"Well done, Peter," he said softly and extended his hand. I shook it absentmindedly while the others looked on—some more shocked than I was, since they hadn't read his letter. I smiled back.

"Looks like the school is going to be able to stay open, then. Thanks, Peter."

"S-so . . . I won?" I asked, still trying to grasp everything.

"Yes, Peter, you did," said Mr. Purvis, looking at Ms. Witherspoon approvingly.

"Of course you did!" said Ms. Witherspoon, giving me a squeeze. "You had the best teacher in the world to tutor you."

"Three cheers for Peter's teacher!" shouted Mr. Larson, who was making his way through the tangle of people on stage. A chorus went up for Ms. Witherspoon. Then everyone cheered for me three times, the school three times, and then three more times because I was alive and hadn't suffered a heart attack from the shock of winning. After the cheering, Mr. Larson shook my hand vigorously and invited me center stage while security worked to get everyone back to their seats so the officials could present me with the check. About then, I thought I saw Mr. Purvis make his way out the ballroom door.

For the presentation, Ms. Witherspoon and my parents stood on my left, and Steven was on my right. The judges came on stage with an oversized check; it had "10,000 Dollars" written on it in huge bold letters. They handed it to Steven and then stepped back.

Steven turned to me and smiled. "For competing so well and still maintaining good sportsmanship, for giving us a tremendous amount of entertainment, and for not killing yourself by falling offstage when you passed out—it is my pleasure as president of the local Christian Businessmen's Association to present you, Peter Paul Pappenfuss, and Davenport Junior

Christian Academy with this check in the amount of ten thousand dollars on this the twenty-second day of October." The crowd thundered its approval as he handed the check to me. It was heavier than I expected, but I held on to it while cameras flashed and a whole sea of people clapped, hollered, and whistled. I couldn't make out their faces, but their silhouettes seemed numberless.

I did make out one silhouette—not because I saw his face, but because the figure was running laps around the ballroom shouting, "WEEEEEE WOOOONNN!" followed by crazed giggling. Sam's Choco-Tacos had finally taken hold of his mind. He probably wouldn't sleep for a week. I laughed as I saw several security guards unsuccessfully try to grab him as he ran along the seats, down one aisle, and up the next. It really added to what was turning out to be quite an experience.

To date, this was the most amazing moment of my life. And although my victory meant that there would be school tomorrow—and every Monday for the rest of the year—somehow I didn't mind. Actually, I couldn't wait, first, because there would be a pizza party for my class, and second, my tutoring sessions would be over. I could enjoy my afternoons again, especially because as long as I held this check, I had a bargaining chip.

"Ms. Witherspoon?" I asked, as the photographers finished up.

"Yes?" she said, looking down at me.

"Is ten thousand dollars enough to buy me out of a couple of weeks of homework?"

"Peter Paul Pappenfuss, are you bribing me to let you out of your studies after winning a city-wide academic contest?"

"Absolutely," I replied. "I heard you need a boiler to stay in business."

She laughed, and Mom and Dad, who overheard, jokingly began blaming each other for the defective genes that caused my behavior. Ms. Witherspoon just ruffled my hair and sighed. "Well maybe if you continue to participate in class like you have been, I'll give you a break."

"It's a deal," I said.

Before we left the Radisson Conference Center, Dad had to fill out a few papers regarding the funds, as well as a release for the local newspaper to feature me and my story. The reporter had already chosen the title of the article: "Contest Winner Passes the Test, Then Passes Out." It wasn't my first choice, but Dad said I should just be thankful for the money and that the whole affair was over. I felt too drained to argue.

While Dad signed papers, I wandered off amid the empty popcorn bags, candy wrappers, and cups. The place was a disaster, and the hotel staff had already begun vacuuming and putting things away. I wanted to find Steven and thank him for putting on the contest and being so supportive. I found him by the stage area, which was being dismantled. He was putting a few papers into an expensive-looking briefcase. He noticed me approaching and smiled.

"Hey there, Peter. Is it starting to sink in yet?"

I shook my head and put my hands in my pockets. "Not really. It probably won't until tomorrow . . . or next semester."

He finished putting his papers away and then stood facing me. "I'm really proud of the way you played the game, Peter, and I'm really glad you won. A lot of these other schools are well off, and it's nice to see God bless people who really have a need."

"Yeah," I said, reflecting on how "lucky" I had been. "God really saved me today."

"Yes, He did. But remember—*even if He doesn't,* He is good, and He will always be there watching over you. I hope you will always dedicate yourself to Him, Peter. I think He has big plans for you."

"That's what my parents keep telling me," I said. Steven smiled warmly in response. "So," I continued, rocking back on my heels, "are we going to do this again next year?"

His smiled faded, and he shook his head. "I'm afraid not, Peter."

"How come?"

"Well, for one thing, it's expensive, but more importantly, I saw some things today that I didn't like."

"Do you mean Milford throwing up? Or the alien sisters in the final round?" He laughed politely.

"Not exactly—but sort of. Peter, I didn't like seeing kids under so much pressure. Even though we advertised this as a friendly contest, people took it so seriously that it strained relationships within families and teachers and churches. I spoke with your father for a bit, as well, and I know that although you have a tremendous support system, you weren't unaffected by the pressures of the contest either."

"I guess so, but it was fun."

"You say that now that it's over. But would you have said that this morning when we first met during the qualifying test?"

I shrugged. "I guess not."

"Don't worry, though, we'll find other ways to give to the local schools. In the meantime, study hard and view this contest as being especially sent by God for you and your school. It came just in time, didn't it? God takes care of us, Peter. Keep putting your trust in Him, OK?" We shook hands, and he left just as Mom and Dad found me.

"Ready to leave, Peter?"

"Yeah—I'm ready. After all, I have school tomorrow."

CHAPTER THIRTY

THE END

Peter, Peter, question-eater,
Had the answer, but couldn't keep her,
It was his turn, and he had to tell,
And he saved our school very well.

"This is awful," I whispered to Harley, who was tapping his feet in time to the music, as he sat in his desk. "I didn't think he could get any worse."

"Come on, Peter," he whispered back, "he's singing about you! You should be honored to have *two* songs composed in your honor."

Echo had arrived just before lunch, making him the tenth visitor to stop by the classroom, so far, to celebrate yesterday's victory. His most recent composition was a cross between a nursery rhyme and whatever his brain could make up on the spot.

"It doesn't make any sense," I complained. "What is he talking about?"

Harley smiled. "You tell me—*you're* the question-eater."

"You're going to be eating my fist, if you keep it up, Harley."

As usual, when the song ended, Echo walked up to me and asked what was my favorite part of the song.

"Um, . . . the end? Again?"

"Right on, man." He held up his fist as a sort of affirmation, and I responded with the same gesture—although I had no idea what I was communicating to him. He left after that, and Ms. Witherspoon shut—and locked—the door.

"OK, class, I think we have had enough visitors for one day. And now, the moment you have all been waiting for. In honor of Peter's victory . . ."

The class applauded, and Calvin, Harley, and Sam slammed their desktops down repeatedly until Ms. Witherspoon whistled loudly to get their attention.

"As I was saying, gentlemen, it's time now for our pizza party. The pizzas should be here in a few minutes. I need Chandra and Lacey to go get the drinks from the cafeteria, along with the plastic forks and spoons."

"Can we use plastic sporks?" asked Wesley.

"We don't have sporks, Wesley," said Ms. Witherspoon.

"Aw, I wanted sporks," he whined.

"You're acting like a spork," muttered Jennifer. Wesley scowled back at her.

"OK, class, this is supposed to be a party. Let's not lose focus here," said Ms. Witherspoon, holding up her hand. Then she motioned for me to come up front. "Since Peter did so well yesterday, I'm going to have him say the blessing."

I made my way to the front and faced my class. They were all smiling at me—except Wesley, who was still stewing about his precious "sporks." There was one empty chair in the front—Lucas's chair. No one knew where he was—too embarrassed or jealous to come, maybe. I said a silent prayer for him before blessing the food and thanking God the contest was over.

The party was a huge hit with ridiculous quantities of pizza and root beer. I sat in the back with Harley and Gretchen, shoving slice after slice of gooey cheese pizza into my mouth. Others did the same. While we ate, people asked me about the contest and what it was like.

"Was that Milford kid sick in the prep room too?" inquired Naomi.

"Yep. You two could have been best friends; maybe you could share a bag someday." Everyone laughed—except Naomi who narrowed her eyes at me and then went back to eating her pizza.

"So, which round was the worst?" asked Melissa, slurping down her second can of root beer.

"The one where the balloons knocked him over," said Wesley.

"The balloons didn't knock him over; it was post-traumatic stress disorder," replied Gretchen. "Wikipedia has a whole section on it; I looked it up last night." Everyone nodded, and Ms. Witherspoon suppressed a laugh.

"Just be careful, Peter," she called out. "You can have flashbacks. And if we play dodgeball after lunch, it's critical that you keep your wits about you. Remember what happened to Lucas last week?" She ended her sentence by staring at Calvin and Jennifer.

"Hey, he deserved it," said Jennifer, sitting up straight in her desk. "Didn't he, Peter?" Before I could answer, Calvin spoke.

"Say, where is that twerp anyway? It figures he would be too chicken to show up today after Peter proved him so wrong yesterday. I don't think he even stayed around long enough to see Peter get the check."

I raised my hand to end the discussion. "I don't want to talk about him today. He has his own issues to work through. It's better if we just leave him alone." It was quiet for a moment. An awkward moment. I looked around for something to change the subject as Ms. Witherspoon began handing out brownies for dessert. When she put one on Sam Feltzer's desk, I had it. He was sitting just next to Harley, Gretchen, and me and was wearing a Band-Aid on his forehead. We had all noticed, too, that he was missing a tooth.

"So, Sam, what did you do to yourself? I don't think everyone knows." Sam lit right up. Ms. Witherspoon groaned and looked like she was seriously considering taking back Sam's brownie.

"Oh, that! Well, did you see me running around the ballroom after you won?"

"I don't think anyone could have missed it," snorted Tommy, wolfing down his brownie. "Last I saw, you were being chased by three security guards as you ran along the empty back row of seats."

Sam nodded proudly. Ms. Witherspoon's cell phone went off, and she stepped just outside the room to answer it, as we continued our discussion.

"Yeah, that's right," Sam said, "only I biffed it on the last chair."

"How?" asked Tommy. "I mean besides the billion Choco-Tacos you had that fueled your insanity."

Sam pushed the rest of his brownie into his mouth—and managed to get most of it inside. Obviously, the brownie was beginning to take over his better judgment, so instead of telling us what had happened the day before, he was going to *show* us.

Sam looked over to the door where Ms. Witherspoon was still talking on the phone and then got up on top of his chair. Placing one foot on the edge of his desk and the other on the highest point of the back of his chair, he gingerly spread his legs apart in a careful balancing act. He grinned at all of us with his missing front tooth—it made him look like he was five years old. Then he gave us the play-by-play.

"Well," he began, shifting his weight and posture so he looked like he was in midstride of a run, "let's say that my desk is the last seat in the row and my chair is the second to last. I was in mid-dash, see?" We all nodded, mindful of Ms. Witherspoon, in case she turned around. Sam continued.

"And as I was reaching out with my foot to the last chair, it slipped on the edge, and I fell forward . . ."

Just then, Harley leaned over and spoke into my ear. "Kick his chair."

"What?"

"Come on, Peter! He'll be fine. He isn't supposed to be standing on his desk, anyway. It would be hilarious, and we could all *see* firsthand what happened last night!"

I shook my head and stood up to leave. Harley grabbed my arm. "Where are you going?" he asked. Then he continued in a whisper, "Come on, Peter, I *dare* you."

"No. Besides, the last time I kicked someone's chair, it sparked a whole series of events that stole every afternoon for three months and filled it with homework. Second, I would feel guilty since God brought me through yesterday unscathed. Third, I have to go to the bathroom from all that root beer."

Harley looked disappointed—and I could empathize. It was a perfect setup, after all, which is why I leaned down and whispered in his ear, "But that doesn't mean *you* can't do it." He gave me a half smile, and I could see the wheels turning in his head, as I left to use the restroom.

After I finished and was high-fived by a line of seventh graders coming back from gym class, I decided to get a drink from the fountain in the hall just outside our classroom. When I rounded the corner, however, it was in use. Mary had the third-grade hall pass and arrived just before I did. She stared at me, but not contemptuously like she usually did.

Further down the hall, Ms. Witherspoon was still on the phone, and I could hear Sam's voice faintly fielding questions about his injury. I guess Harley must have used his better judgment—for once. I walked slowly to the fountain and stood quietly behind Mary. "Hurry up," I said. "I'm thirsty." She looked thoughtful for a moment and then stepped aside for me to go first.

"Congratulations," she said softly. It was the first affirming word she had said since last night.

"Thanks," I replied hesitantly, stepping up to the drinking fountain. After eyeing her suspiciously for concealed weapons, I took several long drinks of water before letting her take her turn. When she finished, she turned to me and spoke—trying to make small talk.

"Is that your party in there?" she asked, nodding toward the classroom.

"Uh-huh."

"Sounds like fun." We stood for a moment considering each other. Then Mary held up her hall pass. "Well, I had better get back to class. This pass is good for only five minutes. Enjoy your party . . . you deserve—"

CRASH!

"Ahhh! My *teeth*!" cried the voice of none other than Sam Feltzer. "Am I bleeding? I'M BLEEDING!" His cries were followed by another crash, several screams, and . . .

Ms. Witherspoon flung her cell phone to the ground, as she whirled around and made a mad dash into the classroom. "Sam! Are you alright? What happened in here? Who did this? Who's responsible?"

A chorus of shouts and conflicting explanations filled the room and the hall. Mary stared coolly at me as the chaos from the classroom reverberated around the school. It wasn't long before Principal Purvis came flying past us and burst into my classroom yelling at everyone to "BEEEEEEE QUIET!"

While the tumult continued in the background, Mary took a step closer to me and looked at me straight in the eye. In her hand, she clenched and unclenched her hall pass. Then she spoke in a serious, but calm, tone. Her look reminded me of the time Mom interrogated me as a suspect in a local domestic disturbance last spring when three of Mary's Barbies decided to commit suicide out of my second-floor bedroom window—in full view of Mary and her friends who were playing in the backyard.

"Peter?" Mary said.

"Yes?" I replied.

"Will you be going to the principal's office this afternoon?"

I glanced down at the mangled hall pass in Mary's grip and thought about what Sam would look like with fewer teeth and about how much trouble Harley was going to be in. Looking back up in her face and smiling, I replied, "Not today."

IF YOU ENJOYED THIS BOOK, YOU'LL WANT TO GET THESE BOOKS, TOO.

What We Believe for Teens
Seth J. Pierce

The best nap Seth Pierce ever had was in church.

"I'm not sure who spoke that day, but their voice had a certain numbing effect on the mind and I fell into a deep sleep. As I was coming to I kept hearing this snorting and heavy breathing, and it seemed to be getting louder. Finally it got so loud I had to open my eyes and look around. . . . There was no more noise, but my eyes met stares of several pious churchgoers who looked as though they had eaten something sour. I turned around and faced forward again, and that's when it dawned on me. I had been woken by my own snoring."

That's Seth for ya. He's honest and willing to share his own embarrassments as he crossed the bridge from old child to young adult. He'll help you understand that our Adventist beliefs aren't about having it all together; they are twenty-eight insights into the loving God who knows you better than you know yourself.

ISBN 13: 978-0-8163-2213-8
ISBN 10: 0-8163-2213-9

Pinch River
Growing up hard and fast on the Michigan frontier
Helen Godfrey Pyke

The logging camp in Michigan was often violent. Sven and his father had sailed to the United States to start a new life. Sven's mother and his siblings stayed behind in Sweden. The camp was often violent. Fights among the men were common. Sven had to act older than he was in order to win the respect of the loggers. It was a mercy that he didn't know what lay ahead.

ISBN 13: 978-0-8163-2250-3
ISBN 10: 0-8163-2250-3

3 Ways to Order:
1. Local—Adventist Book Center®
2. Call—1-800-765-6955
3. Shop—AdventistBookCenter.com